I0823620

SUPERNATURAL CREATURES

SUPERNATURAL CREATURES

MYTHICAL AND SACRED CREATURES FROM AROUND THE WORLD

DK

DK | Penguin Random House

Senior Art Editor Ragini Rawat
Project Editor Upamanyu Das
Project Art Editor Noopur Dalal
Editorial Team Vandana Likhmania, Deeksha Micek, Janashree Singha, Nandini D. Tripathy
Consulting Editor Camilla Hallinan
Art Editor Astha Singh
Assistant Art Editor Abhimanyu Adhikary
Senior US Editor Megan Douglass
US Executive Editor Lori Cates Hand
Picture Researcher Jo Walton
Deputy Managing Editor Sreshtha Bhattacharya
Managing Editor Kingshuk Ghoshal
Managing Art Editor Govind Mittal
DTP Designers Jaypal Chauhan, Nityanand Kumar
Senior DTP Designer Harish Aggarwal
Production Editor Vishal Bhatia
Pre-Production Manager Balwant Singh
Production Manager Pankaj Sharma
Production Controller Joss Moore
Jacket Designer Akiko Kato
Senior Jackets Coordinator Priyanka Sharma Saddi
Jacket Design Development Manager Sophia MTT
DK India Creative Head Malavika Talukder
Publisher Andrew Macintyre
Associate Publishing Director Liz Wheeler
Art Director Karen Self
Publishing Director Jonathan Metcalf

Contributors Lizzie Munsey, Stephen Krensky, Andrea Mills
Lead Consultant Nathan Robert Brown
Consultants Manuel May Castillo, Leanne Holt, Pavel Horák, Salima Ikram, Carolyne Larrington, Ragnhild Ljosland, Marie Rodet, Andrew Ng Hock Soon, David Stuttard, Timothy Topper, Faith Wilson
Sensitivity Reader Sarosh Arif

First American Edition, 2024
Published in the United States by DK Publishing, a division of Penguin Random House LLC
1745 Broadway, 20th Floor, New York, NY 10019

24 25 26 27 28 10 9 8 7 6 5 4 3 2 1
001–339255–Aug/2024

Published in Great Britain by Dorling Kindersley Limited

A catalog record for this book is available from the Library of Congress.
ISBN: 978-0-7440-9879-2

Printed and bound in China

www.dk.com

This book was made with Forest Stewardship Council™ certified paper–one small step in DK's commitment to a sustainable future. Learn more at **www.dk.com/uk/information/sustainability**

CONTENTS

IN THE SKIES 92

BENEATH THE WAVES 108

AMAZING HYBRIDS 132

OUR CHAPTERS
This book is divided into chapters based on themes that relate to type of creature, creature attributes, or where a creature is found. Often a creature could sit in more than one chapter, but we've made the decision to feature it in one chapter or another.

INDIGENOUS STORIES
This book features some Indigenous stories, most of which have been depicted and written with help from Indigenous experts.

INCLUDING EVERYONE
A team of editors, designers, and experts from different nations, cultures, communities, heritages, and experiences have come together to make this book, using lots of lenses and viewpoints in their work. In this book, we have tried to be global in coverage and inclusive in our contents. We have also done our best to be respectful when referring to any beings that come from various world religions and belief systems.

SUPERNATURAL CREATURES

We live in a wonderful world of animals of many shapes and sizes. Science helps us understand nature, but it can't explain everything. For centuries, people have pondered the existence of the supernatural: living things that are not natural, with powers beyond our understanding. Supernatural creatures have been part of our stories for as long as we have been telling them, passed down by word of mouth from storyteller to storyteller. Some look a little like humans or animals, while others are unlike anything you might have seen. This book features just a few of the supernatural beings from around the world. It is hard to prove which of them might or might not be real, so they are all described as if they physically exist.

WHOSE STORY?
We know much more about the stories from the dominant cultures of Europe that colonized other countries. Many of the stories told by the people they oppressed have been lost, but some survive. In this book, DK has tried to find stories from different parts of the world.

SACRED CREATURES
Some of the creatures in this book are sacred to the cultures they come from. But they do have supernatural abilities, which is why they have been featured in this book.

SHARING STORIES

Long before the Internet, phones, movies, or even books, people told each other stories. Huddled around a fire at night, they shared thrilling stories by word of mouth. Over the years, some stories became part of people's cultural identity and beliefs, while others disappeared without trace, long before the invention of writing could put all kinds of stories on the record.

MYTH
An ancient story or set of stories used by early people to explain their world or things they did not understand. Myths have been told for generations, and often feature gods and monsters. Medusa was a snake-haired monster in ancient Greek myths.

LEGEND
A traditional story from the past that cannot be proved to be historical or true. Legends often feature mighty heroes, noble rulers, and fantastic beasts, such as the European wyvern, a type of dragon.

FOLKLORE
A collection of stories, traditions, and beliefs from a particular community. It includes superstitions and beliefs that are hard to prove. Germanic folk stories feature many gnomes.

SACRED BELIEF
Some supernatural creatures are sacred in their cultures. The taniwha is sacred to the Māori people who live in Aotearoa (present-day New Zealand). Their beliefs include many tales about the taniwha.

RELIGION
A system of beliefs involving the worship of a god or many gods. Many religions feature supernatural creatures, including sacred ones. Some creatures help the gods, while others, such as the ancient Egyptian Apep, oppose them.

URBAN LEGEND
A modern-day story that spreads rapidly, often set in a town or city, about something funny or scary. The chupacabra is famous across Latin America.

WHY TELL A STORY?

Long ago, when people rarely left their villages, farms, or hunting grounds, they had limited ways to understand the world around them. So they attempted to explain it through their stories. They wondered how the world began, what made the sun disappear at night, and what half-glimpsed monsters drown fishermen at sea. Supernatural creatures could explain these things.

MORE THAN NATURAL

Sometimes supernatural creatures are versions of things that exist in nature. Japan's Nue has the legs of a tiger, the head of a monkey, the body of a raccoon dog, and a snake for a tail—all of which makes for a bigger and scarier animal.

WHO, WHAT, WHERE

Supernatural creatures often reflect their place of origin. For example, ancient communities of people who hunted and gathered food imagined creatures linked to hunting. Terrifying beings such as West Africa's Sasabonsam, which preyed on unwary humans, dictated where and when people were allowed to hunt.

MISTAKEN IDENTITY

Supernatural creatures may be mistaken versions of real animals. Scottish selkies, who shapeshift between seal and human form, are probably based on actual seal sightings.

THE "UNKNOWN"

If people come across something unfathomable, a supernatural explanation can seem likely. Ancient drawings of large two-legged creatures may be what triggered the modern search for Bigfoot.

UNUSUAL EVENTS

Before science explained them more fully, some people attributed natural events such as earthquakes and tsunamis to supernatural creatures. For example, Japan's kamaitachi are said to cause whirlwinds and dust devils.

ORIGINS

Stories about how the world began are common to most cultures around the world. They may feature supernatural creatures that set creation in motion, such as Auðumbla, the first cow in Norse myths.

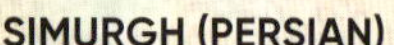

SIMURGH (PERSIAN)

FIREBIRD (SLAVIC)

TWO PLACES AT ONCE

Tales of creatures unique to one region may spread with travelers to other regions, which sometimes leads to similar supernatural creatures in two places. But similar creatures may also develop independently in cultures that have had little or no interaction, such as the Simurgh and Firebird.

PRESERVING STORIES

Thousands of years ago, mysterious beings were depicted in prehistoric rock art. But for much of history, stories have been passed down through word of mouth, before they were recorded in pictures and carvings and then in writing.

NORSE STELE (CARVING ON STONE)

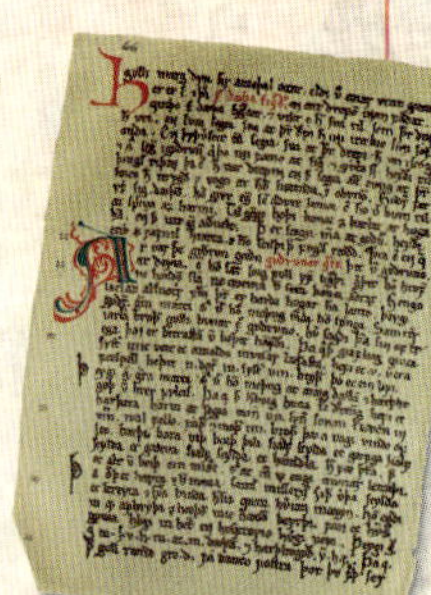

HANDWRITTEN NORSE TEXT

GOOD VS EVIL

Many stories center around an ongoing struggle between the forces of good and evil. The role of evil is generally played by a fearsome supernatural creature, and good by a noble human. However, many stories also feature supernatural beings that represent the qualities of goodness, nobility, and justice.

The Lambton Worm from English folklore is a representation of evil.

A brave knight ends the Worm's reign of terror.

A SENSE OF ADVENTURE

Stories about supernatural creatures have inspired a sense of wonder and a taste for adventure for thousands of years. Cryptozoologists (people who study creatures whose existence has never been proved) have headed to all sorts of remote and dangerous places, in attempts to find these creatures and verify their existence. They have yet to succeed. All too often, a promising new lead turns out to be a false trail, or even a hoax—a tall tale with fake evidence and exaggerated accounts of a supernatural being.

YETI HUNTERS ON AN EXPEDITION TO THE HIMALAYAS IN 1954

GONE BUT NOT FORGOTTEN

Even if evidence of a supernatural creature is debunked, people still enjoy the thrill of the stories that surround it, and flock to see where it was once thought to live. Scotland's Loch Ness monster, for example, continues to attract hordes of visitors, and has inspired a wide range of souvenirs, including plush toys, chocolates, and more. By 2020, Nessie was making more than $51 million for Scotland every year.

The alleged Loch Ness monster, in a 1934 photo

1961 POSTER OF A FRENCH FILM ABOUT WEREWOLVES

1975 BOOK ON THE MOTHMAN

MODERN RETELLINGS

Some stories are recent, such as the ones about Mothman, and others are far older but continue to grip our imagination thanks to modern retellings in books, movies, and other media. Whether people believe in supernatural creatures or not, they're clearly here to stay.

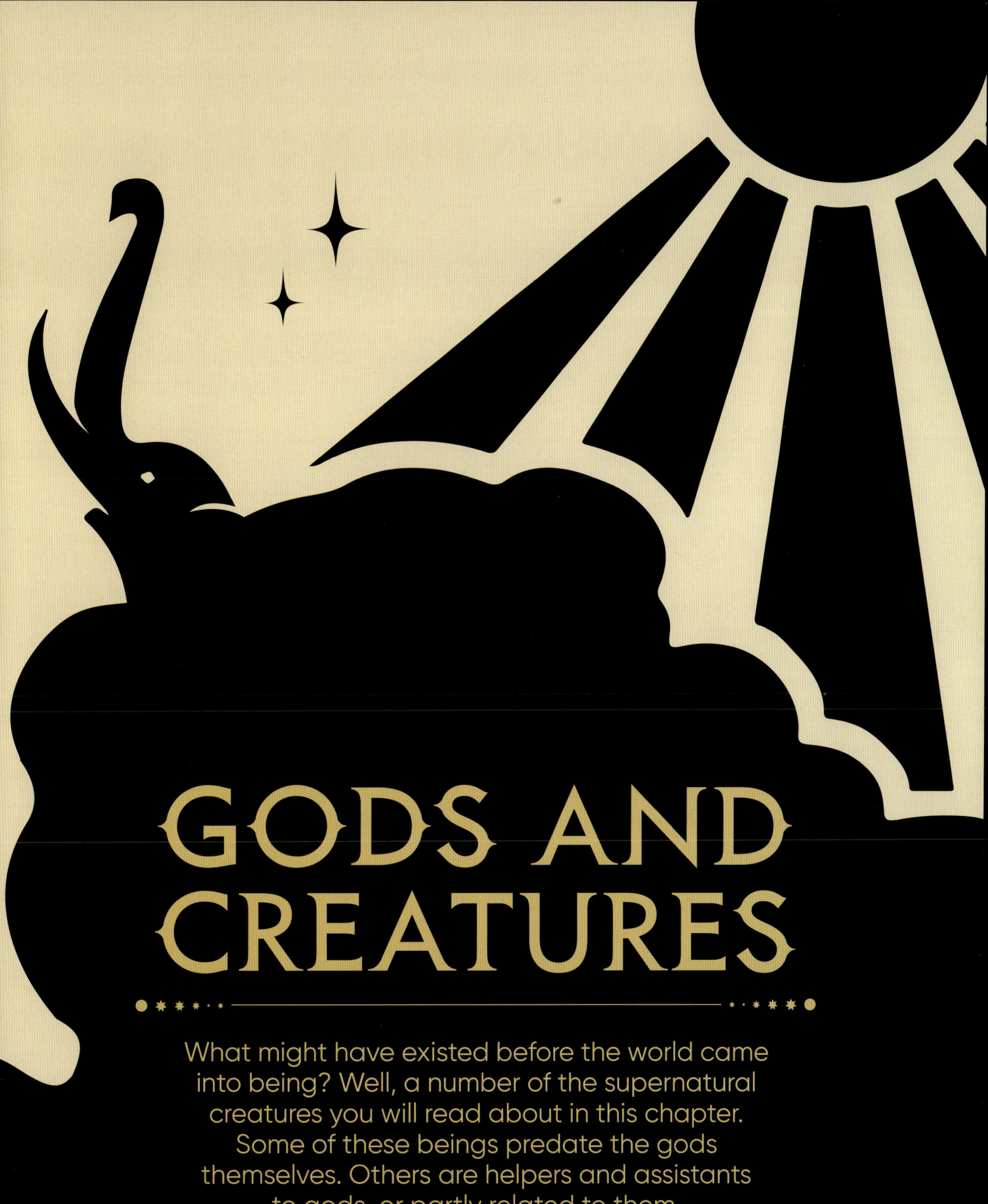

GODS AND CREATURES

What might have existed before the world came into being? Well, a number of the supernatural creatures you will read about in this chapter. Some of these beings predate the gods themselves. Others are helpers and assistants to gods, or partly related to them.

AUÐUMBLA
PRIMEVAL COW

In Norse mythology, the creator and nurturer of the first beings in the universe was a cow called Auðumbla. Before the world began, there was only Ginnungagap, an enormous, empty wasteland where fire and ice collided. Auðumbla spent her time licking the salty ice of this lonely landscape until forms began to emerge. Four rivers of milk spilled from her udders to nurse the first giants and gods as they came to life.

POETIC EDDA
Ancient manuscripts are an invaluable resource for tracing the origins of mythological stories. A great example is the *Poetic Edda*, a medieval collection of anonymous Norse poetry written down in 13th-century Iceland, but dating back to 800–1100 CE.

LIFE GIVER
The warmth of Auðumbla's tongue melts the ice and thaws the first god Buri in this illustration from an 18th-century manuscript of the *Prose Edda*, a retelling of Norse myths and legends, written in the 13th century by Icelandic chieftain Snorri Sturluson.

YMIR
FIRST GIANT

Taking a primordial place in Norse myths is Ymir, the first jötunn (giant), from whom all the giants were descended. As the opposing realms of fire and ice left their mark in the gaping void of Ginnungagap, this frosty colossus grew from drops of running water. He drank Auðumbla's milk to grow stronger. Ymir was the first of many giants to do battle with the gods, with his story told in the ancient text *Poetic Edda*.

MAKING THE WORLD
The gods used Ymir's body to create a new world. His blood turned into the oceans, his flesh became the soil, his hair grew into trees, his brain turned into clouds, and his skull formed the sky.

Odin, Vili, and Ve carry Ymir's skull to make the sky.

Odin and his brothers watch as Ymir's body lies at the center of Ginnungagap.

GIANT KILLERS
The descendants of the first god Buri were three brothers named Odin, Vili, and Ve. These Norse gods killed Ymir to end the terrifying reign of the giants. After Ymir's death, the gods dragged his body into Ginnungagap as seen in this illustration made by American artist Katharine Pyle in 1930.

Ymir's **gigantic bones** became towering mountains.

DECORATIVE ICON
The hippocampus became a common motif in ancient Greece and Rome, and can be seen far and wide on many objects, including ancient coins, Roman bath mosaics, water fountains, Venetian gondolas, and even this ink and gouache artwork from 1807.

HIPPOCAMPUS
OCEAN STEED

Making a splash in ancient Greek mythology is this hybrid sea creature who carries deities across the ocean. The hippocampus has the head and front legs of a horse and the scaly tail of a fish. Its name comes from the Greek words *hippos* ("horse") and *kampos* ("sea monster"). Powering through the water, hippocampi (or hippocamps) can be of great help to those in trouble at sea.

POSEIDON'S CHARIOT
Hippocampi were the trusty steeds of water nymphs crossing the ocean. They even pulled the magnificent chariot of Poseidon (whom the Romans called Neptune), the god of the sea.

GOD OF THUNDER
Raijū can be calm and harmless, but they are closely associated with the god Raijin and stormy weather. As seen in this 17th-century painting, Raijin bangs his drums to make the sound of thunder. In Shintoism, a nature-based religion practiced in Japan, Raijin is the god of thunder.

Trees split by lightning are said to have been clawed by raijū.

RAIJŪ
THUNDER BEAST

If you're outside in stormy weather, remember to lie down on your belly—or raijū might climb into your navel to take a nap. If that happens, Raijin the god of thunder will shoot arrows of lightning to wake up these terrifying creatures from Japanese folklore. Once awoken, they howl with the sound of deafening thunderclaps and punish wrongdoers on Earth. Wherever raijū land, chaos reigns, bringing raging infernos and destroying everything in sight.

Scaly body similar to a dragon

FANGS AND CLAWS
Made of pure lightning, raijū can be disguised as anything from a dragon to a wolf, but they are always armed with vicious fangs and claws. This Japanese illustration from the 18th century shows a dragonlike version.

CERBERUS
HOUND OF HADES

In ancient Greek mythology, ferocious Cerberus is the ultimate guard dog who protects the underworld. This enormous hound guards the gates of the underworld to ensure that the souls of dead people can never escape their fate and living mortals can never enter the underworld without dying. Armed with three terrifying dog heads, snakes protruding from its back, and a serpent's tail, Cerberus deals with the souls foolish enough to try to leave by tearing into them with razor-sharp teeth and devouring them whole.

POISONOUS ACONITE
According to myth, the highly toxic aconite plant was created from the saliva of Cerberus. When the Greek hero Hercules kidnapped Cerberus from the underworld, drops of saliva fell from the beast's mouth and grew into this poisonous flowering plant. For a long time, people used its deadly poison on spears and arrows for hunting and in battle.

Cerberus may come from the Greek **creoboros** meaning "flesh-devouring."

Eighteenth-century marble statue of the god Pluto (the ancient Roman version of Hades) at the Nymphenburg Palace in present-day Munich, Germany

MASTER OF CERBERUS
Cerberus serves as the faithful companion of Hades, immortal god of the underworld. Hades' brother Zeus, king of the gods, gave him Cerberus as a pup. In this statue, the hound sits at the feet of Pluto (or Hades).

This ancient Greek vase painting from the 4th century BCE shows Hercules holding Cerberus on a leash, accompanied by the deities Hermes (left) and Hecate (right).

THE FINAL LABOR
The legendary hero Hercules was given 12 challenging "labors," or tasks, with the final task the hardest of all—he was to capture Cerberus and drag the hound away from its post. Hercules used his amazing strength to wrestle the beast into defeat. When Hercules' mission was complete, Cerberus returned to the underworld once more.

STONY SENTINEL
Terrifying Cerberus stands guard in this stone relief from a Roman mausoleum (tomb) made in the 2nd century CE. When mortals die, their souls travel to the underworld to visit Hades. Only when Cerberus allows them through the gates can the souls be judged, with different fates for heroes, sinners, and ordinary people.

Hugin represents **thought** and Munin stands for **memory.**

ODIN'S SPIES
Perched on Odin's shoulders in this illustration from an 18th-century Icelandic manuscript, Hugin and Munin report everything they have seen and heard during the day. They understand human languages, and can swiftly fly around the world, making them excellent spies for the god.

HUGIN AND MUNIN

ODIN'S RAVENS

On each shoulder of Odin, the All-Father and king of the Norse gods, sits a raven. One is Hugin, and the other Munin. These ravens are no ordinary birds—they are Odin's messengers, bringing him news and carrying out his commands. They are able to cross between Asgard, the realm of the gods, and Midgard—the human realm.

READING RUNESTONES
The ancient Norse people carved letters called runes into stone. Runes were said to hold magic. In the Norse poem *Hávamál*, Odin sacrificed himself nearly to death in order to unravel the mysteries of the runes.

FENRIR

FEARSOME WOLF

An enormous menacing wolf with fiery eyes, Fenrir will bring doomsday itself.

The 13th-century poetry collection *Poetic Edda* reveals the events that will lead to the end of the world, including a colossal final battle called Ragnarök. According to the prophecy, it is Fenrir who will cause mayhem and ignite the conflict. He inherited his huge size and strength from his mother, the giantess Angrboda, and his cunning from his father, the trickster god Loki. No wonder the gods were terrified of him.

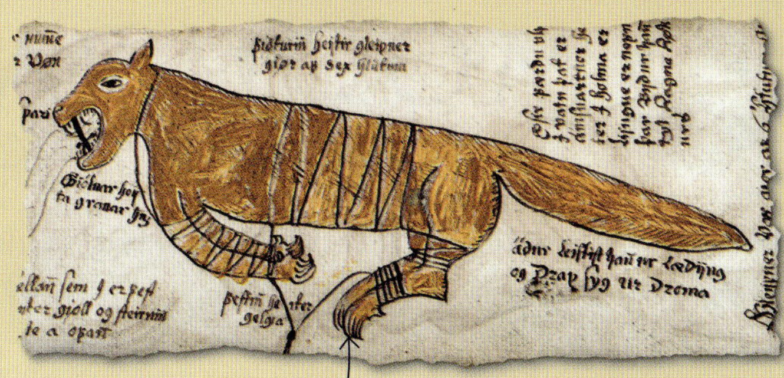

Gleipnir was forged by dwarves deep underground, in their realm called Nidavellir.

BINDING FENRIR

To prevent Fenrir wreaking havoc, the gods had to outwit him. So they challenged him to test his strength, then tied him up using a very strong, specially forged chain called Gleipnir.

Fenrir's brother Jörmungandr fights the gods.

The frost giants help Fenrir fight the gods.

GOD KILLER

The cosmos will end with Ragnarök–vividly depicted in 1885 by German artist Johannes Gehrts. In this battle, Fenrir will break free of his chains and run amok. He is fated to kill the god Odin, and then be slain by Vidar, one of Odin's sons.

MOON RABBIT
HEAVENLY COMPANION

Reach for the moon in some ancient Chinese stories and you'll discover a rabbit hard at work on its surface. The Moon Rabbit is a close companion of the moon goddess Chang'e, who possessed an elixir (or potion) of immortality on Earth. Fearing it would be stolen, she took the potion and fled to the moon, where she stayed forever more, later bringing the Moon Rabbit to give her company. Known by many names, including Jade Rabbit and Golden Rabbit, it spends its time making more of the elixir, pounding the ingredients with a pestle and mortar. Over time, its story spread beyond China, to Korea, Japan, and Vietnam.

Chang'e has snow-white skin and lips the color of cherry blossoms.

ELIXIR OF IMMORTALITY
The lunar creature is brought to life in this spectacular embroidered silk from 17th-century China. The Moon Rabbit stands on its hind legs under a cinnamon tree, making more of the elixir by pounding away at it. In some Japanese stories, the Moon Rabbit simply grinds flour for rice-based cakes called mochi.

MOON GODDESS
As depicted in this 19th-century painting by Japanese artist Tsukioka Yoshitoshi, Chang'e holds the elixir of immortality. In one version of her story, Chang'e was a mortal woman who stole the elixir, drank it to become immortal, and fled to the moon. In another version of the tale, she accidentally consumed the elixir, became immortal, and was transported to the Moon.

MOON FESTIVAL
The Mid-Autumn Festival is a harvest festival celebrated on the 15th day of the 8th month of the Chinese calendar. Family and friends gather to eat delicious bean-paste-filled pastries called mooncakes. They remember this as the day that Chang'e first arrived on the moon.

China's first robotic moon rover was named **Yutu** (Jade Rabbit).

UCHCHAIHSHRAVAS

SEVEN-HEADED STALLION

If two heads are better than one, then this flying horse in Hinduism has a lot going for it with its seven heads. The devas ("gods") and asuras ("demons") churned a primordial ocean in search of *amrita*, the nectar of immortality. One of the treasures that rose from the waters was Uchchaihshravas, the snow-white ancestor and king of all horses. He was claimed by both sides, but he eventually became the steed of Indra, king of the gods.

Surya, the sun god, rides the heavenly steed.

Uchchaihshravas is shown here with fewer than seven heads.

MYTHICAL HORSES

Several horses in ancient myths have extra heads or legs. In Norse mythology, the god Odin rides Sleipnir, his eight-legged steed. It was depicted by the Vikings on this stone from Gotland, Sweden, around 700–900 CE.

The stallion's name means "neighing loudly" in Sanskrit.

CHARIOT OF THE SUN

Uchchaihshravas pulls the chariot of the sun god in this brass lamp from India, made in about 1900. As a divine horse, he has the strength to draw the mighty vehicle across the sky. In some versions of Surya's story, his chariot is pulled by seven horses.

DIVINE MOUNT
Airavata appears in different Southeast Asian cultures, including Hindu, Buddhist, and Jain beliefs. In this 19th-century painting from Gujarat, India, he carries the god Indra, who sits in front of his wife Shachi and the infant Jain savior, Jina Rishabhanatha. In this version, Airavata is shown with a single head and three trunks.

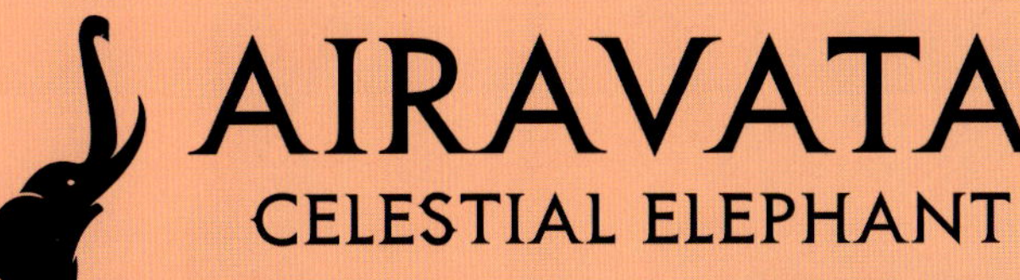

AIRAVATA
CELESTIAL ELEPHANT

Rarest of all white elephants is this magnificent, many-headed creature made by Brahma, the Hindu creator God. Airavata is the king of the elephants. He carries Indra into battle, and guards his palace in Svarga ("heaven"). One day, when the sage Durvasa gave the god a garland, Airavata threw it on the ground. Furious at this insult, the sage cursed the devas with mortality. To save themselves, they had to find the nectar of immortality (see page 24).

Erawan uses his trunks to deliver water from heaven to Earth.

MIGHTY ERAWAN
In Thai beliefs, Airavata is known as Erawan, who has three or sometimes 33 heads. This three-headed statue comes from the province of Songkhla, Thailand.

MEDUSA
GRUESOME GORGON

Turn away from Medusa's terrible gaze or you may turn into stone! On an island not far from Greece lived three monstrous sisters known as gorgons. One of them, Medusa, could turn people into stone with a glance. The sisters all shared an unusual feature: instead of hair, coils of hissing snakes spiraled out from their heads. Medusa's two sisters—Stheno and Euryale—were immortal, but sadly for Medusa she did not share this trait and met her end at the hands of the hero Perseus.

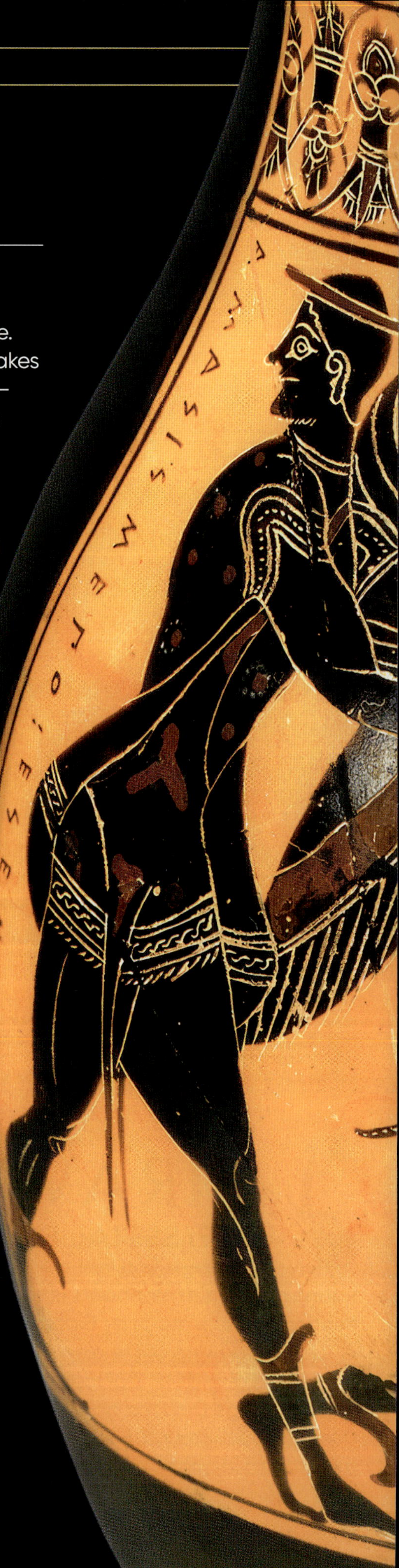

DEATH BY DECAPITATION
Medusa is shown as a monster, with wings and tusks in addition to her snake hair in this piece of pottery from around 550 BCE. She was killed by the legendary hero Perseus, who had been sent on a mission to collect her head. Here his face is turned away from her, protecting him from her fatal gaze as he finishes the deed. Perseus then wielded Medusa's head as a weapon, using it to turn his enemies to stone.

BORN BEAUTIFUL
In one version of her tale, Medusa is a beautiful maiden led astray by the sea god Poseidon in the goddess Athena's temple. Enraged, Athena cursed Medusa, turning her into a gorgon. This carved stone shows Medusa as a beautiful woman before her transformation.

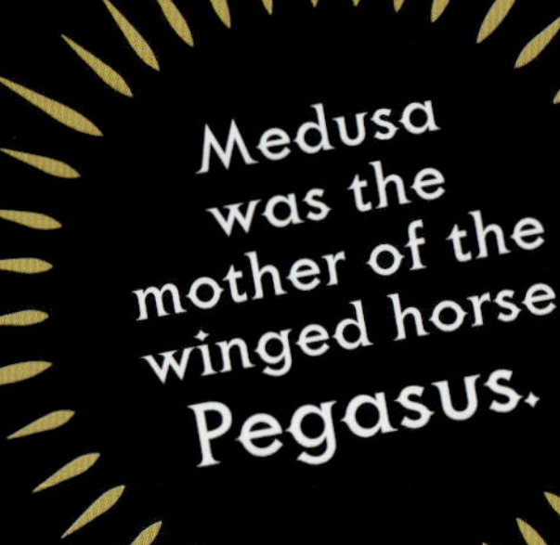

GORGON ON STAGE
Medusa's tale is still popular in the arts today. She appears in stories and even on stage—this image is from a ballet, *Medusa*, which premiered at the Royal Opera House in London, UK, in 2018. Modern versions of Medusa's story are more likely to portray her as a powerful woman than a monster.

The god Hermes watches as Perseus kills Medusa.
The snakes on Medusa's head were venomous.

Ra uses a knife to slay Apep.

NIGHTLY BATTLE
Taking the form of a cat, Ra battles Apep each night on his way through Duat. Every night, he manages to kill the serpent, only for Apep to reappear and fight him again the next night. Their battle is shown here in a wall painting from the tomb of Nekhtamun, in Deir el-Medina, Egypt.

APEP
DARK SERPENT

In ancient Egyptian mythology, the sun god Ra's archenemy is Apep, who represents darkness and chaos.
Depicted in art as a giant serpent, Apep is said to be 48 ft (15 m) long, with a head made of flint. It encircles the world and seeks to destroy life, order, and peace—everything that Ra stands for. As Ra sails his great barge through Duat ("underworld") every night, Apep attempts to kill him, but fails repeatedly.

Apep's diet includes **human souls.**

LAMASHTU
DEADLY DESTROYER

The bringer of sickness, disease, and death, Lamashtu struck fear in the hearts of many. The daughter of the Mesopotamian sky god Anu, Lamashtu was a rebellious demigoddess who was cast out of heaven. She had a woman's body, an eagle's legs, and a lion's head. This terrifying hybrid ate men, killed children, harmed pregnant mothers, kidnapped newborn babies, and created as much misery and devastation as possible.

MENACING MONSTER
Lion-headed Lamashtu grips a pair of serpents in her claws and suckles wild beasts as she stands on a donkey in this stone amulet from around 800–550 BCE. Amulets such as this one were hung up to ward off Lamashtu.

BABYLONIAN EPIC
Named after its human hero, *Atra-hasis* is Mesopotamia's earliest epic poem. Written in the 18th century BCE in Babylon (in present-day Iraq), it was recorded on many clay tablets, such as this one from around 1630 BCE. It reveals how parents began singing lullabies to babies to prevent them from crying and attracting the attention of evil deities such as Lamashtu.

HELPING HEPHAESTUS
Hephaestus was the god of fire and blacksmiths in ancient Greece. According to some writers, he was assisted by the cyclopes who toiled away in his forge, turning hot metal into superb armor, weaponry, and jewelery for the gods. This image shows Vulcan, the Roman version of Hephaestus, at his forge with the cyclopes.

CYCLOPS
ONE-EYED GIANT

Meet cyclops, the human-eating monster. This creature belongs to a lawless race of giants (the cyclopes) who devour people in tales from ancient Greece. Huge and colossally strong, they have just a single eye in the center of the forehead. In some accounts, they are outcasts and cave dwellers, with no respect for the gods and no fear of heroes.

ESCAPING POLYPHEMUS
The brutish cyclops Polyphemus is frozen in time in this marble sculpture from the 2nd century BCE. When the Greek hero Odysseus was stranded on Polyphemus's island, this cyclops started eating his crew. To escape, Odysseus blinded Polyphemus with a poker in his only eye.

The cyclopes forged the thunderbolts of Zeus.

TYPHON
MEGA MONSTER

The monster of all monsters in ancient Greek mythology was terrifying Typhon. He was a formidable sight, with giant limbs made of hissing serpents, fire-filled eyes, and poison dripping from his mouth. His ability to breathe fire and trigger typhoon winds made him virtually invincible. Although he failed to overthrow the Olympian gods, he left a lethal legacy as the father of many evil monsters to follow.

BATTLING ZEUS
Typhon fights the Olympian god Zeus in this scene depicted on an Athenian vase from 490 BCE. When Zeus hurled his thunderbolts at Typhon, the monster finally fell, proving that Zeus was now the supreme deity in ancient Greek mythology.

Coiled serpents make up Typhon's lower body.

Typhon's burial place under Mount Etna is shown in this copper engraving from 18th-century France.

VOLCANIC EXILE
In most myths, Typhon was defeated and buried under Mount Etna in Sicily, Italy. It is said that every time this volcano explodes, it is really the full force of Typhon still trying to escape.

Typhon's children include **Chimera and Cerberus.**

SPIRITS AND DEMONS

Spirits are ghostly beings that do not have physical bodies. Many of them choose to live in a particular place, such as a forest, lake, or cave. They range from kind and good all the way to dangerous and downright evil. Those at the evil end of the scale are known as demons.

ATTENDING THE GODS
While they are not goddesses themselves, nymphs are often linked closely to gods and goddesses. In ancient Greek myths, nymphs often appear as attendants to several gods, including Hermes—as seen in this detail on a Greek vase from the 6th century BCE.

CALYPSO AND ODYSSEUS
When the legendary hero Odysseus washed up on the shores of Ogygia, the nymph Calypso trapped him on the island for seven years. Odysseus longs for escape in this 1924 illustration by Scottish artist William Russell Flint.

NYMPH
NATURE SPIRIT

Take a close look at a pool of water or a tree and you may catch a glance of a beautiful nymph. Nymphs are spirits linked with natural features such as mountains, woods, rivers, and springs. These spirits have magical powers and long lifespans, and care for the well-being of the place with which they are associated. Nymphs first appeared in myths in ancient Greece, and were rediscovered by Renaissance artists.

The dryad holds a branch from her tree.

Marble sculpture

If a tree dies, so might a dryad.

WOOD NYMPH
Italian artist Carlo Pittaluga created this sculpture called *Nymph of the Woods* in 1915. Woodland nymphs are called dryads, and each dryad has her own individual tree. If the tree is harmed in any way, the dryad feels its pain.

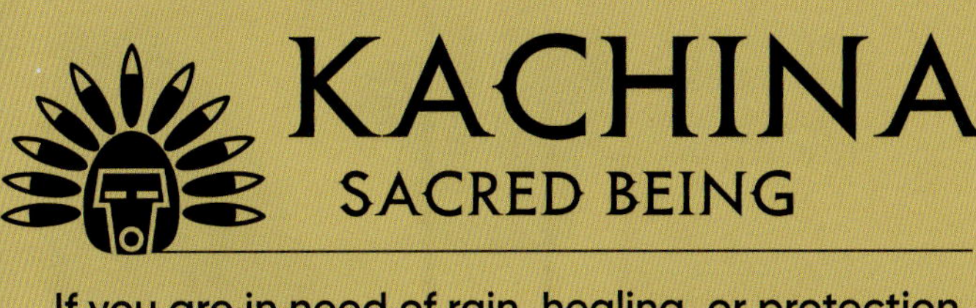

KACHINA
SACRED BEING

If you are in need of rain, healing, or protection, a kachina might be able to help you.
In the religion of the Hopi people living in the southwestern US, kachina are powerful spirits representing many things in the natural world—from particular places, crops, animals, and seasons to dead ancestors and the sun. Kachina only allow themselves to be seen when a particular ritual is performed by people wearing a kachina mask—then the spirit depicted on each mask temporarily takes over the performer's body.

There are hundreds of kachina.

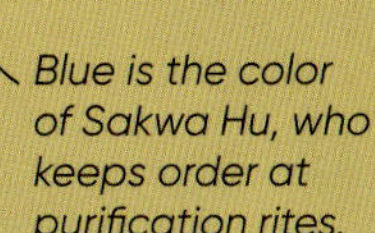

Blue is the color of Sakwa Hu, who keeps order at purification rites.

Sakwa Hu carries a whip made of yucca leaves in each hand.

RITUAL RETURN
Each February, many Hopi villages carry out a ceremony called *Powamu*, in which the men perform a set of rituals. The ceremony celebrates the annual return of a kachina to a village, and marks the beginning of the bean-planting season.

HOPI CRAFT
The Hopi people are known for their skilled craftwork. This young Hopi artist is carefully painting a traditional kachina doll. The Hopi also excel at making textiles, jewelery, baskets, and clay pots.

KACHINA DOLLS
Children are given kachina dolls to teach them about Hopi beliefs. This blue and bearded doll, made by Hopi artist Tom Callateta, represents Sakwa Hu, the Blue Whipper who punishes people when they misbehave.

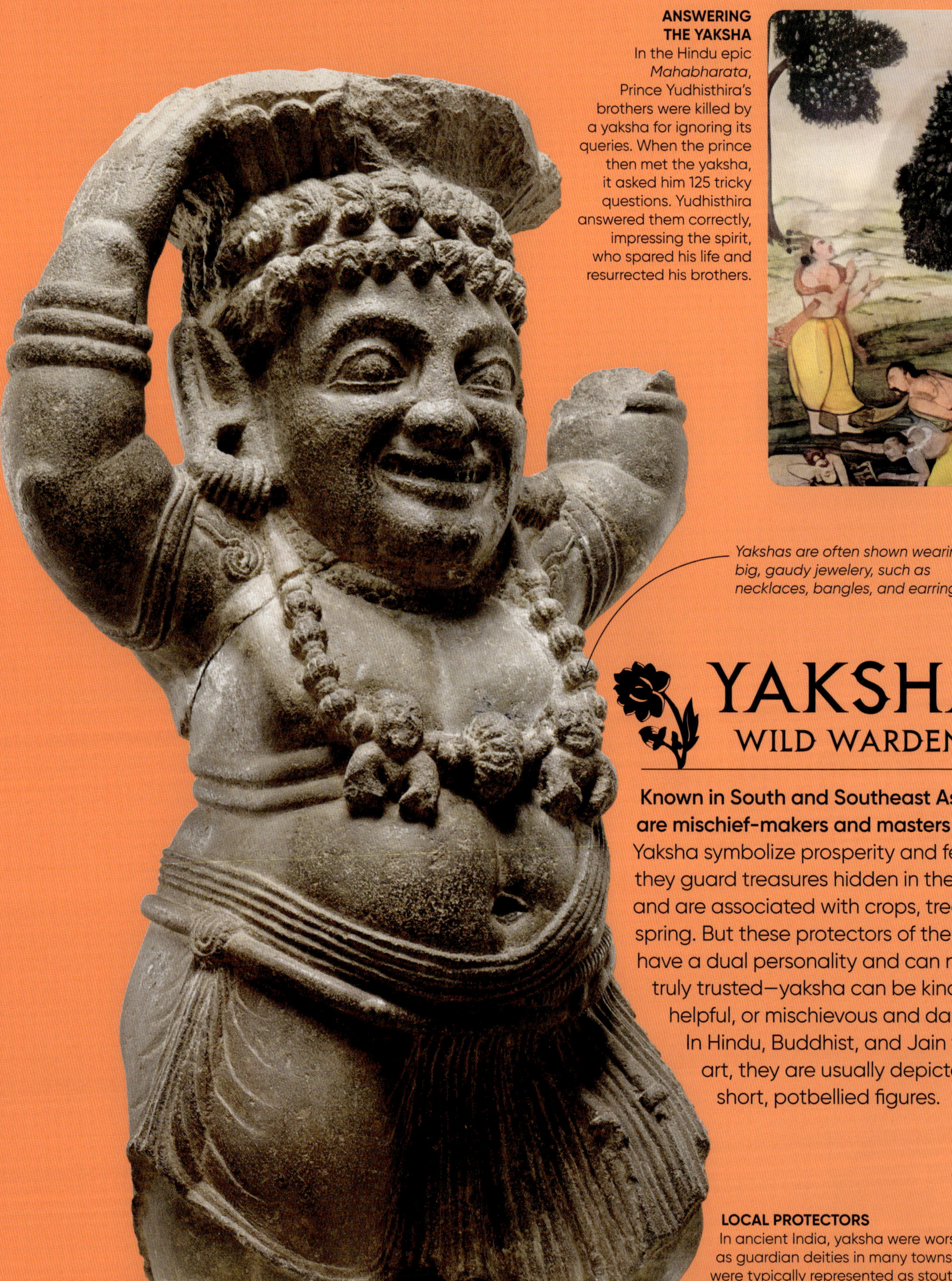

ANSWERING THE YAKSHA
In the Hindu epic *Mahabharata*, Prince Yudhisthira's brothers were killed by a yaksha for ignoring its queries. When the prince then met the yaksha, it asked him 125 tricky questions. Yudhisthira answered them correctly, impressing the spirit, who spared his life and resurrected his brothers.

Yakshas are often shown wearing big, gaudy jewelery, such as necklaces, bangles, and earrings.

YAKSHA

WILD WARDEN

Known in South and Southeast Asia, yaksha are mischief-makers and masters of magic. Yaksha symbolize prosperity and fertility—they guard treasures hidden in the earth, and are associated with crops, trees, and the spring. But these protectors of the wilderness have a dual personality and can never be truly trusted—yaksha can be kind and helpful, or mischievous and dangerous. In Hindu, Buddhist, and Jain texts and art, they are usually depicted as short, potbellied figures.

LOCAL PROTECTORS
In ancient India, yaksha were worshipped as guardian deities in many towns. They were typically represented as stout figures, like this Buddhist sculpture, made around 100 BCE. It was found in the Pitalkhora Caves in Maharashtra, India.

DAY OF THE DEAD
Each November, the annual *Día de los Muertos* ("Day of the Dead") in Mexico honors loved ones who have died. People come together to enjoy feasts and parades, including this spectacular show about La Llorona staged in Mexico City.

BEWARE HER CRIES
The story of La Llorona sees her condemned to walk the earth, wailing for her lost boys and absorbed by her own grief. She is inextricably linked to children, from her own dead sons to young children she may lure to their deaths.

A crying La Llorona has been carved into this tree in Coahuila, Mexico.

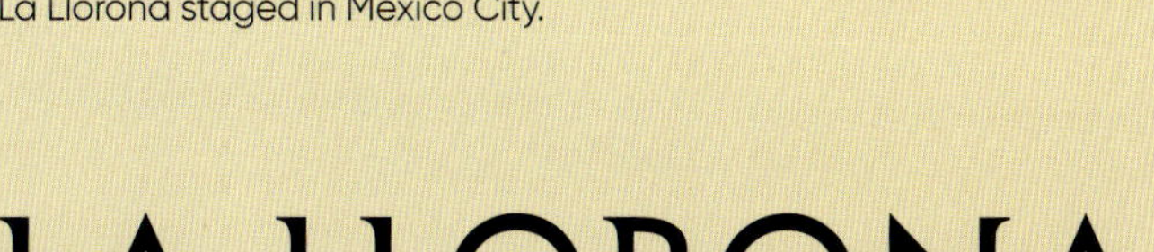

LA LLORONA
WEEPING WOMAN

The mournful cries of this tortured spirit echo through Mexican mythology.
La Llorona voices her grief around waterways where it is said she drowned her sons in a fit of rage at her unfaithful husband before taking her own life. Although the story's details may vary, her haunting presence remains the same, and anyone who hears her can expect grave misfortune to follow. This terrifying tale is often told to children to encourage them to stay close and to avoid dangerous waters.

WHITE LADY
Strange female spirits appear in similar tales from many countries. French folklore describes dame blanches ("white ladies") as spirits that loiter outside homes to warn people of impending death, and wander along pathways to torment travelers. In Ireland, too, the cry of a banshee means death is close by.

VODYANOY
THE ONE IN THE WATER

The vodyanoy of Russian and other Slavic folklore in Central and Eastern Europe is a vindictive water spirit who looks like an old man clothed in murky green slime.
Accounts vary from one region to another, but vodyanoys generally have a frog-like face, a long white or green beard, webbed paws, and a fishy tail. When a vodyanoy gets angry, he destroys dams and mills, floods crops, and drowns animals and people. Farmers and fishermen try to keep him happy by leaving food and other offerings, but it doesn't always work.

A vodyanoy is also known as **vodník** in some countries.

CUP OF SOULS
The vodyanoys prize teapots as their most valuable possessions and collect fine porcelain teacups with lids, like this one from 19th-century Russia. They use them to store the souls of people they drown.

With his long beard, the vodyanoy is often nicknamed "Grandpa Waterman."

This vodyanoy can shape-shift into human form.

WATERY MENACE
It's sunset in this early 20th-century illustration by Russian artist V. V. Vladimirov. That's when the vodyanoy emerges from the depths, imitating human sounds to lure people into his watery lair. Some say he uses his victims as helpers in an underwater palace.

SLASHING SPIRAL Kamaitachi are so fast, they're invisible, especially at night. This one, illustrated by Japanese artist Sekien Toriyama, comes from *Gazu Hyakki Yagyō* ("The Illustrated Night Parade of One Hundred Demons"), first published in 1776.

KAMAITACHI

WOUNDING WEASEL

This yōkai's name means sickle weasel.

If you suddenly get caught up in a whirlwind at night, watch out—three yōkai (monsters) called kamaitachi are about to attack.

In Japanese folklore, the kamaitachi are speedy weasels that work in teams of three. As they pass by on the wind, the first weasel makes you stumble, the second one cuts you, and the third puts a numbing ointment on the wounds to delay the pain. It's all over in a flash. Only later do you notice the cuts, which are rarely fatal.

ONI
WICKED DEMON

Caves and mountains can be far more dangerous than they appear—they may be home to fearsome oni. Most of these creatures live in hell, where they torture souls. But many gigantic oni live alongside us on Earth, never missing an opportunity to inflict their wickedness on humans. All oni are roughly human in shape, but demonic in nature. They have horns, sharp teeth, muscular bodies, and strangely colored skin. Oni appear in Japanese myths, where they are known for their malicious nature.

HELLISH AFTERLIFE
In Japanese Buddhism, hell is called Jigoku. After death, the world's most evil people are sent there to be punished by oni, who work for Enma (right), the king of hell.

COLORFUL SKIN
Oni are usually shown with blue, pink, white, or red skin. Blue and red are the most common colors. This blue oni is from a Japanese scroll painting created in 1764.

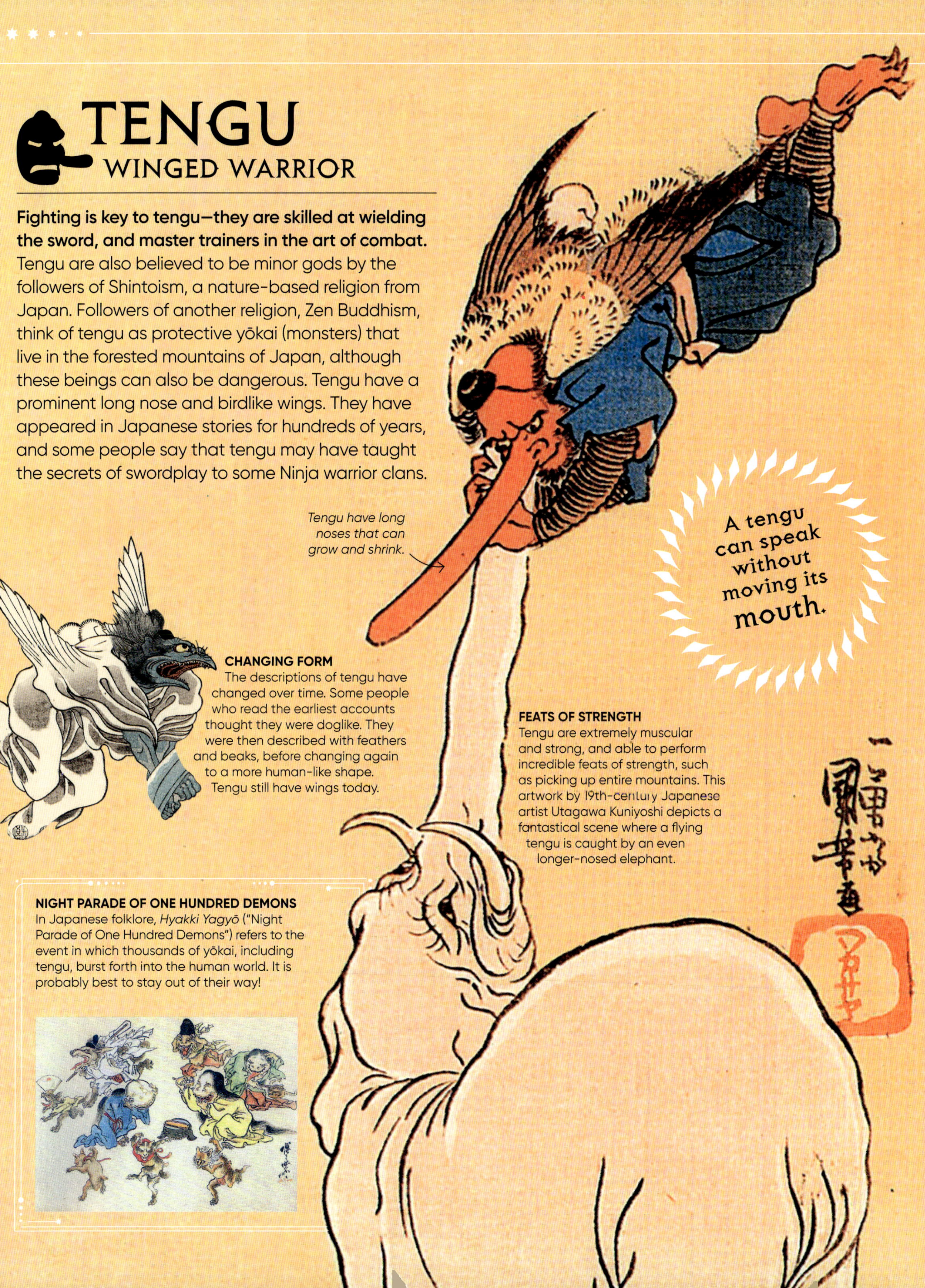

TENGU
WINGED WARRIOR

Fighting is key to tengu—they are skilled at wielding the sword, and master trainers in the art of combat. Tengu are also believed to be minor gods by the followers of Shintoism, a nature-based religion from Japan. Followers of another religion, Zen Buddhism, think of tengu as protective yōkai (monsters) that live in the forested mountains of Japan, although these beings can also be dangerous. Tengu have a prominent long nose and birdlike wings. They have appeared in Japanese stories for hundreds of years, and some people say that tengu may have taught the secrets of swordplay to some Ninja warrior clans.

Tengu have long noses that can grow and shrink.

A tengu can speak without moving its mouth.

CHANGING FORM
The descriptions of tengu have changed over time. Some people who read the earliest accounts thought they were doglike. They were then described with feathers and beaks, before changing again to a more human-like shape. Tengu still have wings today.

FEATS OF STRENGTH
Tengu are extremely muscular and strong, and able to perform incredible feats of strength, such as picking up entire mountains. This artwork by 19th-century Japanese artist Utagawa Kuniyoshi depicts a fantastical scene where a flying tengu is caught by an even longer-nosed elephant.

NIGHT PARADE OF ONE HUNDRED DEMONS
In Japanese folklore, *Hyakki Yagyō* ("Night Parade of One Hundred Demons") refers to the event in which thousands of yōkai, including tengu, burst forth into the human world. It is probably best to stay out of their way!

DEMONS
MASTERS OF MALEVOLENCE

Among the most deadly creatures in mythology are demons. These vicious beings are the catalyst for violence and chaos. Over the centuries, they have taken the form of evil gods, corrupt sorcerers, and wicked sinners. They might also be ghosts of the dead, creatures from hell, or corrupt hybrids on Earth. But all serve as agents of evil.

DIV-E SEPID
In the mythology of Persia (present-day Iran), the chieftain of all demons was called Div-e Sepid ("white demon"). He used magic to create deadly storms. In this 16th-century illustration, he battles the Persian warrior Rustam.

Mephistopheles is often described as wearing a red cape.

HANNYA
A distinctive mask of an angry female demon has been worn in the Japanese tradition of Noh theater since the 16th century. The hannya represents the soul of a woman who was jealous in life, and transformed into a horned devil after death.

MEPHISTOPHELES
In German folklore, a trickster demon named Mephistopheles works for the Devil by leading the damned to Hell. Yet he also warned Dr. Faust that selling his soul to the Devil for a life of knowledge and pleasure will make him the Devil's eternal slave.

Aghasura's body remained where he died, with village folk crossing it as they went about their day.

AGHASURA
This powerful demon in Hindu beliefs transformed into a super-size serpent with a gaping mouth to eat innocent people. As seen in this 18th-century painting, Krishna—the human avatar of the supreme God Vishnu—entered his mouth to kill him.

Aghasura's snakelike body was 8 miles (13 km) long.

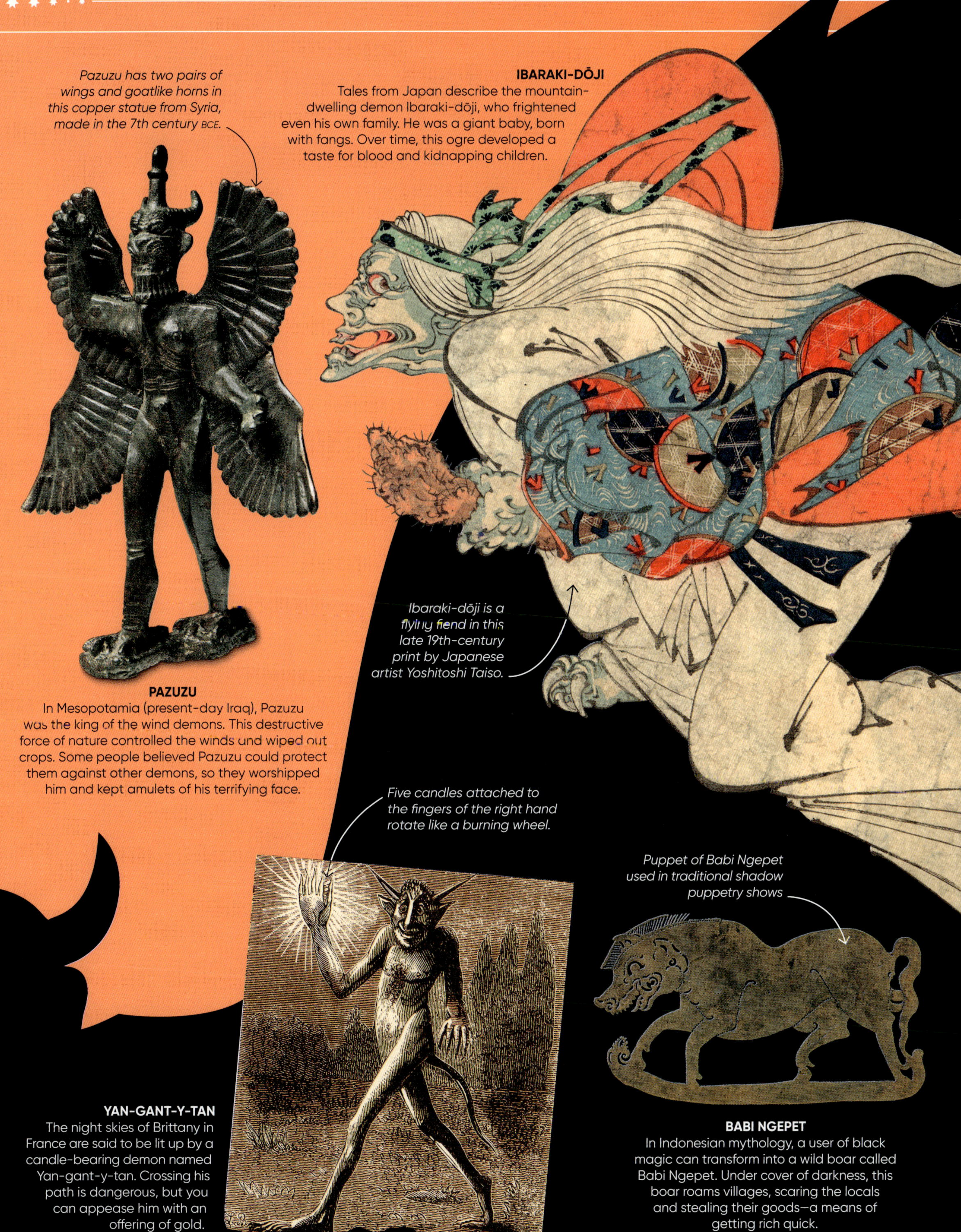

Pazuzu has two pairs of wings and goatlike horns in this copper statue from Syria, made in the 7th century BCE.

IBARAKI-DŌJI

Tales from Japan describe the mountain-dwelling demon Ibaraki-dōji, who frightened even his own family. He was a giant baby, born with fangs. Over time, this ogre developed a taste for blood and kidnapping children.

Ibaraki-dōji is a flying fiend in this late 19th-century print by Japanese artist Yoshitoshi Taiso.

PAZUZU

In Mesopotamia (present-day Iraq), Pazuzu was the king of the wind demons. This destructive force of nature controlled the winds and wiped out crops. Some people believed Pazuzu could protect them against other demons, so they worshipped him and kept amulets of his terrifying face.

Five candles attached to the fingers of the right hand rotate like a burning wheel.

Puppet of Babi Ngepet used in traditional shadow puppetry shows

YAN-GANT-Y-TAN

The night skies of Brittany in France are said to be lit up by a candle-bearing demon named Yan-gant-y-tan. Crossing his path is dangerous, but you can appease him with an offering of gold.

BABI NGEPET

In Indonesian mythology, a user of black magic can transform into a wild boar called Babi Ngepet. Under cover of darkness, this boar roams villages, scaring the locals and stealing their goods—a means of getting rich quick.

ONAM
Some asuras are revered in parts of India. The annual festival of Onam is celebrated in Kerala, India, to honor King Mahabali, ruler of the asuras. The *Theyyam* ritual is a major highlight of the event. It combines music and dance, featuring performers in elaborate, colorful costumes and makeup.

Male performers wear body paint and large headgear when representing King Mahabali.

ASURA
DEADLY DEMON

A fearsome asura is a powerful demon from Hindu beliefs that stands against the devas ("gods"). The asuras live in Patala ("hell"). They are proud, boastful, stubborn, and quick to anger. These wicked warriors desire power and seek to conquer all realms and worlds. And even though they are in constant conflict with the gods, who live in Svarga ("heaven"), the asuras are actually related to the devas. The Creator Brahma's son Kashyapa married the sisters Aditi and Diti. Diti gave birth to the asuras, while Aditi was mother to the devas.

Asuras are usually depicted with blue-green or deep red skin.

Many of the devas wear golden crowns into battle.

The word **asura** first appears in the Vedas, Hindu texts from 3,500 years ago.

These smaller versions of Raktabija grew from the drops of his blood that spilled on the ground.

ETERNAL CONFLICT
The asuras and devas have always been at odds, which has led to some epic battles. This early 19th-century Indian painting shows their two armies charging at each other on horses, elephants, and other steeds. At one point, the two sides forged a temporary alliance to retrieve *amrita*, the nectar of immortality (see page 24)—but it was broken when the asuras were cheated by the devas, who kept the nectar for themselves.

MULTIPLYING MONSTER
In their quest for power, some asuras spent long periods of time praying to one of the three Supreme Gods: Brahma, Vishnu, or Shiva. Pleased with their devotion, these Gods granted them their wish. Shiva gave the powerful asura Raktabija the ability to create versions of himself from his blood spilled in battle. Armed with this ability, Raktabija wreaked havoc—he is seen mid-fight in this 19th-century illustration from an ancient Hindu text called *Markandeya Purana*.

AKVAN AND RUSTAM
A powerful div called Akvan could turn invisible or into a raging storm. But this wasn't enough to worry the Persian hero Rustam (see page 101). In this illustration from the 10th-century epic poem *Shahnameh*, Rustam looks unconcerned as Akvan prepares to throw him into the sea. He will survive the ordeal and return to defeat the div.

DAEVA
CREATURE OF CHAOS

In ancient Iran, this giant demon with horns, claws, and tail was bent on destruction. A daeva is evil personified, and causes chaos. Daevas originated in Zoroastrian beliefs, which may have portrayed them as former gods rejected by their followers. They were later called divs in epics from Persia (present-day Iran), where they often traveled at night, ruining the lives of people they met.

CHIEF OF DAEVAS
This stone relief from Apadana Hall in Persepolis (in present-day Iran), made around the 4th century BCE, shows the daeva chief Angra Mainyu killing a bull. In some versions of his origin story, Angra was the evil son of Ahura Mazda, the supreme god of Zoroastrianism.

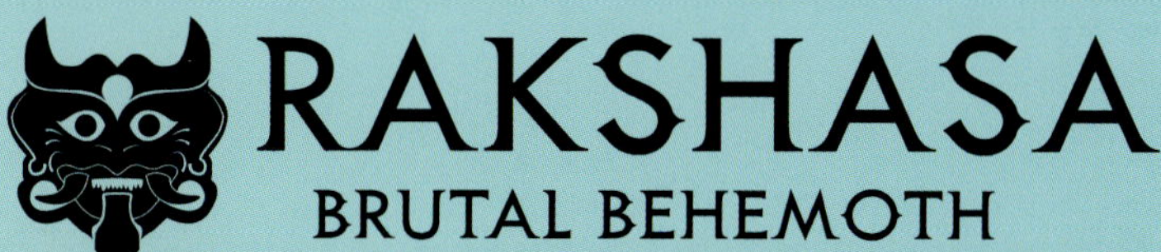

RAKSHASA

BRUTAL BEHEMOTH

Even the eyebrows of a rakshasa are scary, and that is on top of its monstrous size, fanged teeth, poisonous fingernails, and terrifying glare. Rakshasas are monsters who can fly and shape-shift into any form that suits their purpose, which often includes eating human flesh. In Hindu beliefs, most rakshasas are warriors on the side of evil, and they are at their most powerful at night.

CHANGING PERCEPTION
Although many rakshasas are now seen as evil in India, in the past, people believed that some rakshasas were scholars. Over time, these beings became more demonic-looking in Indian manuscripts, as seen in this 19th-century illustration of the rakshasa Kumbhakarna fighting Rama's army.

As a prince of the wealthy realm of Lanka, Kumbhakarna is often depicted wearing jewels.

A rakshasa has the power to create illusions.

A monkey soldier struggles in Kumbhakarna's crushing grip.

RAGING WARRIOR
In the Hindu epic tale *Ramayana*, the legendary prince Rama fought against the demonic Ravana in Lanka. Ravana's brother, a rakshasa warrior called Kumbhakarna, fought alongside him. In this conflict, Rama's monkey army attacked Kumbhakarna, but were no match for his monstrous power. Monkey warriors swarm over the enraged rakshasa in this statue at the Uluwatu Temple in Bali, Indonesia.

MAGICAL BEINGS

Supernatural creatures defy the everyday laws of nature, with bodies and abilities that can't be explained by science. The following pages feature just a few of the many creatures that are often associated with the incredible powers of magic.

Elaborate colors and ornate gold detail

FIRE BREATHER
The dragonlike head, scaly skin, and oversize horn of the qilin can be seen in this 18th-century statue. Although peaceful by nature, the qilin becomes angry if provoked and breathes fire in the face of evil.

The qilin walks on clouds to avoid hurting grass.

Each foot has four claws.

QILIN
BEAST OF FORTUNE

Count yourself lucky if you cross the path of the qilin. This dragonlike creature is very elusive, but brings great fortune to anyone who sets eyes on it.
A sacred animal in Chinese mythology, the qilin has appeared only in pivotal moments in history, marking the birth or death of a benevolent ruler or a wise scholar. Some say a qilin was spotted at the birth of the Chinese philosopher Confucius, highlighting his future importance.

Head shaking is typical of the qilin dance.

FESTIVAL DANCE
The qilin is honored every Chinese New Year. Performers dress up as it and imitate its movements to the sound of traditional music.

UNICORN

ONE-HORNED MARVEL

Brought to life in many favorite fairy tales, the unicorn is considered the most magical of beasts. A fleeting glimpse is the best you can hope for with the fast-footed unicorn. This white, horselike animal has a single, spiral horn with spellbinding power and immense healing properties. The first unicorns were depicted in early art from Mesopotamia (present-day Iraq), before the creature emerged in European folklore as a guardian of the forest.

ANCIENT ANIMAL
The unicorn has crossed cultures for centuries. This 4,000-year-old engraved seal from the Indus Valley shows an unidentified animal with a distinctive horn. Similar depictions of one-horned creatures have been made by some other cultures.

PURE AND GOOD
Unicorns gained popularity in medieval European art. Woven in Flanders, France, around 1500, this tapestry, *The Lady and The Unicorn,* shows a noble maiden and a unicorn with a twisted horn, goatee, and lion's tail. Only young maidens could tame unicorns because they both shared the same virtues of purity, goodness, and grace.

YAMATA NO OROCHI
In Japanese folklore, Yamata no Orochi was an enormous, eight-headed, eight-tailed dragon. Following the beast's reign of terror, it was finally slain by Susanoo, the god of seas and storms.

This dragon's body was the size of eight valleys.

German aquamanile (water vessel) shaped like a wyvern

DRAGONS
CHAOS AND LUCK

The definition of a dragon depends on where you are in the world. In many European myths, dragons are feared as fast-flying, fire-breathing monsters hellbent on causing chaos. Legendary heroes often battle these creatures. But in many Asian cultures, dragons are celebrated as smooth-moving serpents that may bring good luck. They are protectors in control of life-sustaining water and rain. From benevolent to malevolent, here are some dragons that have made their mark on mythology and belief around the world.

WYVERN
Popular in European folklore and British heraldry, a wyvern has two scaly legs, two wings, and a tail ending in a poisonous stinger. However, some think that a wyvern is not a dragon at all!

Stained glass window in St. Gwyddelan's Church, Wales

Sculpted figure from the Ishtar Gate, Babylon, to protect the city against invaders

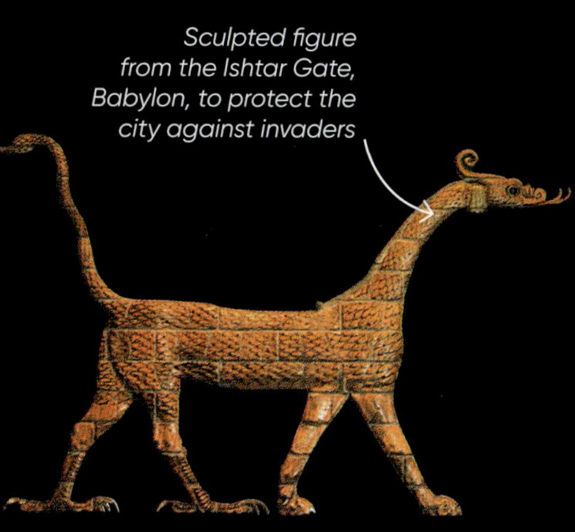

Y DDRAIG GOCH
Meaning "the red dragon," Y Ddraig Goch is seen throughout Wales, from the national flag to the St. David's Day parade. It first emerged during the reign of King Cadwaladr around 655–682 CE.

MUŠḪUŠŠU
This dragon from Mesopotamia (present-day Iraq) has a serpent's head, the front legs of a lion, and the back legs of an eagle. It protects locals and brings good fortune.

YONG
A long, thin Korean dragon, the Yong may stretch 50 ft (15 m) from end to end and has a flowing white beard. This wise, water-dwelling beast controls the rain and brings good luck.

Decorative depiction of Druk in a Bhutanese street mural

Dragons were first mentioned in the myths of Mesopotamia.

ZMEY
In Slavic mythology, zmey (or zmei in Russia) started out as a serpent but grew into a dragon, and could also turn human. Sometimes shown with many heads, this weather dragon can cause droughts or floods on a whim.

Druk represents wealth, and is often shown holding precious stones.

DRUK
The thunder dragon, or Druk, is a national symbol of Bhutan, and features on its flag. It is strong yet serene, and keeps company with Tibetan monks.

CHINESE DRAGON

BENEVOLENT PROTECTOR

Huge, snakelike bodies and sharp claws make ancient Chinese dragons look threatening, but those who are pure of heart have nothing to fear from them.

Also called "Lóng," dragons from ancient China are noble beings representing wisdom and power. They protect people from harm and bring good luck to those around them. With power over air and water, these dragons can control rivers, seas, and the weather, bringing rain to places suffering from drought and stopping floods. For thousands of years, they have played important roles in myths and folklore across China.

DRAGON KINGS
The most powerful dragons in Chinese mythology are four brothers collectively known as Longwang, or the Dragon Kings. These guardian deities are linked to the seasons and to the seas around China, and sometimes appear in a humanlike form. They are Ao Guang, Ao Ru, Ao Shun, and Ao Quin.

CHASING PEARLS
Ancient Chinese dragons are often shown in pairs, chasing after a pearl, as seen in this illustration on a porcelain dish from the Qing period (1644–1912). The pearl represents power and prosperity. Dragon pearls are said to be able to make people's wishes come true.

Five claws on each foot means this is an imperial dragon—lesser dragons have four claws.

In China, every twelfth year is the year of the dragon.

DRAGON DANCE
An elaborate dragon dance is often the highlight of Chinese New Year celebrations. The dragon is a huge puppet, which is controlled by a team of dancers. They use poles to make the dragon dance through the streets, timing the wavelike movements of its body to the beats of drums. The longer the dragon, the more luck it brings.

Eastern dragons don't have wings.

THE POWER OF DRAGONS
In imperial China, dragons were often used as a symbol of royal power. The emperor's throne was known as the "Dragon Throne." This portrait shows the Empress Dowager Cixi (1835–1908), who ruled China for nearly fifty years. She is known as the "Dragon Lady."

EUROPEAN DRAGON

FIERY DESTROYER

With fire streaming from its mouth and huge wings beating through the sky, a dragon makes for a terrifying sight. Stories about dragons have been told in Europe for centuries, all the way back to Typhon, father of the dragon that guarded the Golden Fleece in ancient Greek mythology. These fearsome beasts have huge scaly bodies with thick skin. In medieval legends, dragons often feature in battles that are symbolic of the struggle between good (a warrior) and evil (a dragon).

The Greek word *drakon* means "serpent".

DARING DRAGON SLAYER
For medieval warriors, slaying a dragon was the ultimate test of bravery. A dragon's skin is hard to penetrate, so the most effective way to kill it was by throwing a lance into its open mouth, as seen in this 15th-century painting called *St. George and the Dragon*.

GUARDING TREASURE
Dragons are said to guard hoards of precious treasure—huge mounds of gold, jewelery, and valuable items. To keep the treasure safe, the dragon sits right on top of it, and spits fire to burn any thieves to cinders. In many European folk tales, these beasts live deep under mountains or inside caves with their prized troves.

St George, the most famous dragon slayer of all time

POPULAR CHARACTERS
A dragon burns enemy wagons on a road in the TV series *Game of Thrones*. European dragons frequently appear as characters in books, films, and television shows from around the world. These dragons of today still have the same features as their medieval ancestors.

MISCHIEF-MAKERS

TRICKS AND PRANKS

What fun would magical powers be, if they didn't let you be a little bit naughty?
Many stories mention creatures with mischievous tendencies. Some of them pull pranks that are largely harmless, or just for fun, while others have far more evil intentions, and may even kill. Here is just a small selection of the rascally creatures found in folk stories from all over the world.

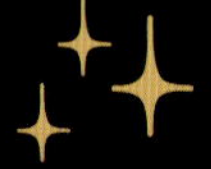

HOBGOBLIN
These small and grotesque creatures appear in stories from many parts of Europe. Some are simply mischievous, while others are far more wicked, and are often inclined to steal. Keep an eye on your gold!

TOKOLOSHE
This small water spirit from South African folklore can make itself invisible by drinking water or swallowing a stone. It likes to scare, and can cause illness or death. A spiteful person might call upon a tokoloshe to create problems for others.

ELF
If you venture deep into a European forest, you may come across an elf. These magical creatures live for a very long time. If they get involved with people, they may choose to create problems—or to help them out.

LEPRECHAUN
Ireland is home to leprechauns—little humanlike beings that may have big beards. They love gold and are famous for their skill as cobblers (shoemakers). Leprechauns might help people or hinder them, depending on their mood.

IMP
Small, wild, and willful, these little demons love to dance and play pranks. Imps are found in England and Germany, and aren't all that evil, despite being demons. They're really just very naughty.

A single eye sits in the center of the forehead.

HITOTSUME-KOZŌ
The hitotsume-kozō is a Japanese yōkai (monster) that likes to appear suddenly, giving people a shock. It looks like a child with a bald head and a single eye, and its favorite food is tofu (bean curd).

Leprechauns earn their gold by fixing shoes of fairies.

Brownies are often shown sweeping.

ALUX
Dwarflike alux spirits can be found in the Yucatán Peninsula in Mexico. They are usually invisible, but appear in person if they want to frighten humans. An alux can spread disease and cause chaos, but it can also guard a sacred site.

BROWNIE
Want a hand with your household chores? If you live in Scotland or England, you could try asking a brownie. However, if you give them clothes, they will prank you and never help again.

Seven kindly dwarves feature in the Germanic fairy tale of Snow White.

DWARF
Dwarves are short and strong, with long beards. They often live deep inside mountains and mines, and are skilled metalworkers. Some are kind, some mischievous, and some very serious. You'll find all kinds in stories in Norse and German folklore.

Twelve butterflies draw the airborne carriage.

Sprites can ride **birds** as well as butterflies.

SPRITE STRUCK
A number of natural weather events are named after mythical creatures, including elves, gnomes, pixies, and sprites. The rare phenomenon called sprite lightning appears high above a thunderstorm as flashes of red lightning.

SPRITE

ETHEREAL SPIRIT

Many western European stories are full of sprites—tiny, brightly colored beings, with beautiful insect-like wings.

These delicate, fairylike creatures use what they can find in their forests to clothe themselves and furnish their homes, shaping leaves into hats and using acorn shells as cups. Their bodies glow faintly at night, which is why people often mistake them for fireflies. Treetop sprites turn fall leaves, shake winter snow off branches, and protect new growth, but not all sprites are helpful. Some water sprites drown sailors, and air sprites can blow fierce storms.

SPRITE ON STAGE
In English playwright William Shakespeare's play *The Tempest*, Ariel is a sprite. He has incredible magical powers, but he is the helper of a sorcerer called Prospero. In this 19th-century illustration, he sings to Ferdinand, a young prince shipwrecked by a storm of Ariel's making.

This sprite has harnessed a flock of butterflies.

A queen of sprites rides in a carriage made of a flower.

RESTLESS FAIRIES
Sprites are small and swift, like buzzing insects, and often stick together to form large swarms. They enjoy bothering butterflies, just for fun. They are also reported to use butterfly-powered transportation, as seen in this 1870 illustration by English artist Richard Doyle.

FAIRIES
A TOUCH OF MAGIC

You may not have seen them, but fairies are all around us. With sightings around the world, fairies pop up in the folklore of many regions and cultures. They are also known as fay, fey, faerie, and fair folk. Fairies come in a range of shapes and sizes, from balls of light to small, winged beings. But all fairies have magical powers—some use it for good, while others prefer to cause harm, and might even kidnap people and carry them off. These pages feature just a small selection of the world's best-known fairies.

PERI
Myths from Persia (present-day Iran) feature the peri. These beautiful, winged fairies were said to be evil in Zoroastrian beliefs. Some people think they can cast love spells. Seen here is a peri in an illustration from a mid-16th century manuscript from Bukhara (in present-day Uzbekistan).

MENEHUNE
Indigenous Hawaiian beliefs describe the menehune, found in remote forests in Hawai'i. They are short, secretive, and good at crafts, such as stone carving and building ponds to trap fish.

TUATHA DÉ DANANN
These Irish fairies, who were once gods, conquered ancient Ireland and are often depicted as kings, queens, warriors, and healers. They are excellent at magic, and never age or become sick. They can also shape-shift and control the weather.

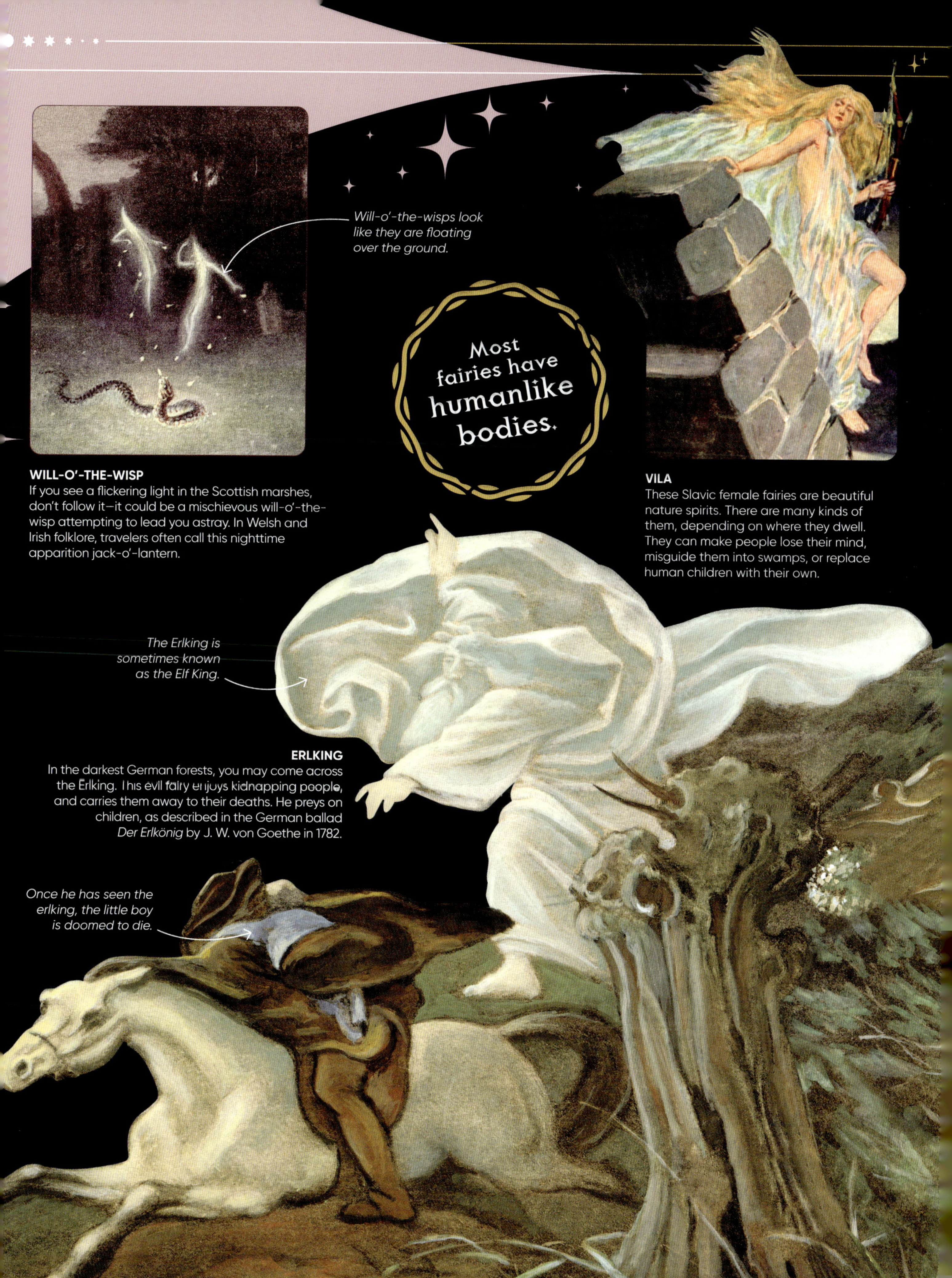

Will-o'-the-wisps look like they are floating over the ground.

Most fairies have humanlike bodies.

WILL-O'-THE-WISP
If you see a flickering light in the Scottish marshes, don't follow it—it could be a mischievous will-o'-the-wisp attempting to lead you astray. In Welsh and Irish folklore, travelers often call this nighttime apparition jack-o'-lantern.

VILA
These Slavic female fairies are beautiful nature spirits. There are many kinds of them, depending on where they dwell. They can make people lose their mind, misguide them into swamps, or replace human children with their own.

The Erlking is sometimes known as the Elf King.

ERLKING
In the darkest German forests, you may come across the Erlking. This evil fairy enjoys kidnapping people, and carries them away to their deaths. He preys on children, as described in the German ballad *Der Erlkönig* by J. W. von Goethe in 1782.

Once he has seen the erlking, the little boy is doomed to die.

DOKKAEBI

PLAYFUL GOBLIN

The good news is that the Korean dokkaebi isn't evil. However, it can be dangerous—if a dokkaebi becomes angry with someone, it probably wants revenge. Most dokkaebi have blunt horns, big eyes, and more hair than they really need. They like to play pranks when they get the chance. They also challenge travelers to a traditional Korean wrestling match called *ssireum*.

MUSOK
A traditional religion from Korea, *musok* is still practiced widely in South Korea. Followers who excel at its rituals are called *mudang*. Dressed in traditional robes, they seek help from gods and ancestors, praying and making offerings to aid people—including those possessed by supernatural beings such as a dokkaebi.

ANCIENT TILE
A dokkaebi towers over the landscape on an ancient clay tile found in Buyeo, South Korea. It was made during the time of the Baekje Kingdom (18 BCE–660 CE), one of the Three Kingdoms of Korea.

The hungry squirrel is more interested in the acorn than the pixie right behind it.

Pixies often look like small people, and have large, translucent wings.

PIXIE

MAYHEM MAKER

Pixies are not the biggest, strongest, or most powerful of the magical fairies, but quite a lot of them roam the British countryside. They have pointed ears and pointed hats, and they like to wear green to blend into their forest surroundings. They are not always friendly creatures—some are known to steal children, and many delight in mischievously leading travelers astray.

A pixie is called a pigsy in southwest England.

TROUBLESOME SPIRITS
A naughty pixie sneaks up a tree branch in the hope of driving a squirrel away in this illustration from the 1924 *Blackie's Children's Annual*. Pixies love to dance in the moonlight, accompanied by a woodland chorus of crickets and frogs.

PIXIE DAY
This celebration takes place annually in Ottery St. Mary, in Devon, UK, on a Saturday in June. On Midsummer's Day in June 1454, church bells drove pixies out of town. Children now dress as the pixies being forced to leave.

TROLL
FOREST FIEND

If you go down to the woods, watch out for terrifying trolls with an appetite for humans.
For centuries, Scandinavian mythology has told tales of monstrous human-like beings who lurk in the dark in forests, caves, and mountains, ready to pounce on their next victim. While some trolls can be as small as a goblin, most are gigantic, and all of them have a grotesque appearance with bulging noses, scruffy hair, and gray skin. Trolls wander by night because sunlight turns them to stone, so children are warned to come home before dark.

Muted colors of the hair, skin, and clothing camouflage the troll in the forest shade.

Trolls are scared of any light, even lightning.

TROLLS IN ART
Trolls have been a popular subject for Scandinavian artists. Swedish illustrator John Bauer imagined a world of forest trolls and other supernatural folk where he lived, and brought them to life in more than 50 artworks. In *The Boy and the Three Trolls* (right) from 1915, he shows three trolls waiting as their mother asks a princess to marry one of her sons.

TROLL'S TONGUE
Scenic landscapes can take the name of mythical creatures said to dwell there. Norway has this dramatic outcrop named Trolltunga ("Troll's tongue") 2,300 ft (700 m) above Ringedalsvatnet Lake. Legend has it that a troll exposed to sunlight was transformed into this rock formation forever.

SCRUPULOUS SPIRITS
Heinzelmännchen ("little men") are a type of kobold from the German city of Cologne. In this 19th-century illustration, they are busy making a mayor's coat overnight, to help a poor tailor.

KOBOLD
HIDDEN HELPER

Tiny, humanlike kobolds enjoy making mischief, but they can also be helpful.
Some live in people's homes, others down mines or even on ships. If there is a kobold in your house, you should keep it well fed—happy kobolds will help out with household chores. Unhappy ones might hide tools or kick you as you bend over. Although they're invisible, kobolds feature in folklore across Germany and northern Europe.

KOBOLDS AT SEA
Ocean-going kobolds are called the klabautermänner. They are expert sailors, and can check ships for leaks or predict if a storm is coming. A klabautermann will also warn the crew if their ship is about to sink.

MYSTERIOUS LOOKS
No one is certain what a boggart looks like, though it is usually described as being small and goblin-like, as seen in this 2017 sculpture by British artists Victoria Morris and Lee Nicholson.

This woodland boggart's toothy, malicious grin shows it's up to no good.

A boggart should never be **named** as it might turn unruly.

BOGGART
SAFETY HAZARD

If you've been having strange problems around your house, you might have a boggart in residence. These creatures appear in old English folklore. They often live in people's homes, and enjoy making life difficult for the occupants, particularly by waking them up in the night. Once a boggart moves in, it's impossible to get rid of. But hanging a horseshoe over the door may stop it from entering your house in the first place.

GNOME
EARTH DWELLER

Since the 19th century, these little fellows have brought good luck as popular figurines decorating gardens across Europe. But delve deeper and you'll discover a more complex creature. Like the dwarves from Germanic mythology, gnomes are tiny guardians of nature, living under the earth. They watch over gold and other treasure, and protect the land and its flora and fauna. But these mischief-makers pop up from underground burrows at night to play tricks on people.

FAIRY TALE FAVORITE
In fairy tales, gnomes are knowledgeable beings skilled in magic who usually help the hero, punish wrongdoing, or warn of trouble. This English fairy tale illustration from the 19th century shows a gnome with a wizened face and a long white beard, dressed in the colors of nature.

There are more than 25 million garden gnomes in Germany alone.

Toadstools deep in the woods are a favorite spot for a gnome to perch.

RENAISSANCE FAME
Gnomes became popular in the 16th century, particularly through the writings of the Swiss alchemist and Renaissance thinker Paracelsus. He described how they could travel through solid earth, like fish through water.

CALIFORNIA GOLD RUSH
When gold nuggets were discovered in California in the 1840s, it set off the California Gold Rush—thousands of people arrived in the region, eager to make a fortune. Armed with shovels and pans to dig for precious gold, they brought about a boom in the mining industry. The folklore of miners also flourished, and tales of characters such as the tommy-knocker endure to this day.

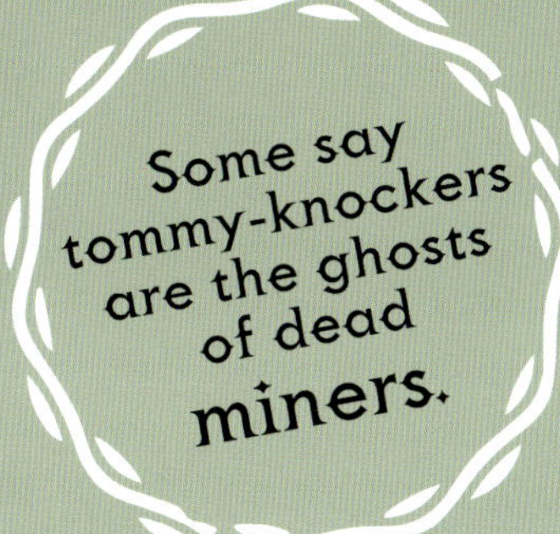

TOMMY-KNOCKER
THIEVING ROGUE

A mysterious underground knocking sound could be a tommy-knocker making itself heard. These legendary imps originated in southwestern England's Cornish tin mines, where they were said to tap on the walls in the darkness. Their story crossed the Atlantic with miners who migrated to the US in the 1820s. Superstitious miners feared these noises as an omen of death, or hoped they were about to strike gold. The stories vary by region, with tommy-knockers ranging from harmless, prank-playing guardians of the mines to dangerous thieves and harbingers of doom.

A lamp illuminates dark tunnels as two tommy-knockers escape with their stolen coal cart.

PRACTICAL JOKERS
Tommy-knockers are only about 2 ft (60 cm) tall, with gnarly skin and faces covered in white whiskers. Their underground home is perfect for practical jokes—these pranksters often extinguish miners' lights and steal their tools. They may even run off with precious coal, as seen in this painting.

MANY VERSIONS
Kallikantzaroi appear in the folklore of many countries, including Greece, Bulgaria, and Türkiye (Turkey). They are usually described as having a mix of human and animallike features, as seen in this Greek depiction.

FESTIVE NIGHTMARE
Many monsters come out at Christmas. One peculiar creature from Icelandic folklore is the Jólakötturinn ("Yule Cat"). This giant feline with glowing eyes roams the countryside looking for people to devour, especially children who don't wear the new clothes they received for Christmas.

DESSERT DEFENSE
One way you can keep kallikantzaroi away is to place a bowl of loukoumades out on the rooftop. This is a dessert from Greece that looks like a doughnut. The goblins will devour this delicacy instead of wreaking havoc in your home.

KALLIKANTZAROS

TRICKY TROUBLEMAKER

Most people look forward to Christmas as a time of joy and goodwill. But not a kallikantzaros. These small, goblin-like troublemakers usually spend their time deep underground, sawing away at the trunk of the world tree that supports our planet, hoping to make it fall. But during the 12 days of Christmas, from December 25 to January 6, they come to the surface every night to make mischief—hiding or stealing belongings, ruining food, and scaring livestock.

GOLEM
CLAY GIANT

A golem is a living statue, formed of dust or earth that has been shaped by a sorcerer. The golem is brought to life in a very particular ritual, in which certain Hebrew letters are written on paper and placed in its mouth or written on its forehead. Usually golems are created to help the sorcerer, or to defend a Jewish community under attack. However, golems can also endanger the people around them—they are prone to breaking free from their creators and causing havoc.

A golem is like a **robot,** with no mind and no soul.

THE GOLEM OF PRAGUE
Originally a movie prop, this clay statue stands at the entrance to Prague's Jewish quarter. It represents the golem created by Rabbi Loew to protect the city's Jewish community from anti-Semitic attacks.

Hebrew letters can be seen on the golem's forehead.

Rabbi Loew stands before the golem he has created.

BROUGHT TO LIFE
In the 16th century, Rabbi Judah Loew of Prague, Bohemia (now Czechia), used clay from the banks of the Vltava River to build a powerful golem. He brought it to life using incantations and Hebrew letters forming a sacred word.

GOLEM GAMES
Mythical characters from long ago often star in modern fantasy video games, too, such as *Minecraft* and *Dungeons and Dragons*. Seen here is Jagara Colossus, a golem character from the fantasy board game *Golem Arcana*.

OMEN OF DEATH

If you hear a banshee lament, then you or a member of your family may be close to death. The banshee's cry is often the first sign of what's to come. The banshee may be dressed in a hooded cloak, as seen in this illustration from Thomas Crofton Croker's 1825 book *Fairy Legends and Traditions of the South of Ireland*.

A barn owl screech may be the closest sound in nature to a banshee.

Armed with a spear, the Morrígan is ready for battle.

MEET THE MORRÍGAN
This 1905 illustration from the book *Celtic Myth and Legend* shows the Morrígan, an Irish goddess of war. She often shape-shifts into a crow, a bird associated with banshees. Her role is to foretell doom and death on the battlefield.

The Morrígan urges warriors to fight and strikes fear into their enemies.

BANSHEE
WAILING WOMAN

The bloodcurdling scream of a banshee is awful to hear—especially if the person hearing it is sick. Women keening (wailing in lament) is a traditional part of funerals in Ireland, Scotland, and many other cultures. But the banshee makes her gruesome shriek when someone is about to die. These beings from Celtic myths have long, unkempt hair and eyes red from weeping. They usually take the form of an aged hag, a murdered woman, or a younger woman who died in childbirth.

WASHING CLOTHES
In France, female spirits called Les Lavandières (washerwomen) are often associated with banshees as omens of death. They are doomed to wash clothes for all eternity, as a punishment for sins committed when they were alive. As seen in this 1861 painting by French artist Yan' Dargent, they wash the clothes of those about to die on a moonlit night. In Ireland, too, the Morrígan washes the clothes of warriors who will die in battle.

The washerwomen are often dressed in white.

When the washerwomen catch a man named Postik spying on them, they break his arms.

LOUHI
WICKED SORCERESS

Watch this powerful, shape-shifting sorceress take to the skies as an enormous eagle.
Louhi is the antihero in a Finnish epic poem, the *Kalevala*, which describes how the world was created and then follows the adventures of several heroes. She has great powers that she uses to steal the moon, the sun, and fire itself. She can also control the weather, whipping up terrifying storms at sea.

Louhi rules **Pohjola,** a land to the north of Finland.

FIGHTING FOR THE SAMPO
Finnish artist Akseli Gallen-Kallela painted this scene in 1896. It shows Louhi engaged in a vicious battle with a group of Finnish heroes who had stolen a powerful magical artifact called the Sampo from Louhi.

BABA YAGA
MAGICAL MENACE

If you are unlucky enough to come across Baba Yaga in the forest, you may end up with your flesh in her stew pot and your bones in her walls. Baba Yaga looks like a harmless old woman, but she is actually a powerful sorceress with a taste for human flesh—and she particularly enjoys eating children. In stories from Russia and central Europe, she sets near-impossible tasks for her victims, then eats them when they fail.

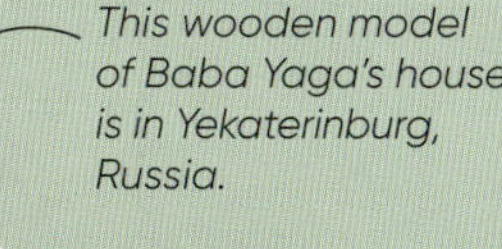

This wooden model of Baba Yaga's house is in Yekaterinburg, Russia.

MONSTROUS HOME
Baba Yaga lives in an extraordinary house. Made of bones, it spins around on an enormous pair of chicken legs and bounces through the forest, wherever she commands.

Baba Yaga carries this giant pestle for steering and a broom for clearing her path.

ANCIENT SORCERY
Sorceresses have appeared in stories and myths for thousands of years. Some use their magic to help and heal, while others use it for evil. The first recorded sorceress was Hecate, ancient Greek goddess of sorcery. She was often depicted with three bodies, as in this Roman statue from the 2nd century CE.

FOREST LIFE
In Russian folk tales, the old sorceress lives deep inside the forest. She flies around in a magical mortar and pestle. This image was created in 1900 for a story about Baba Yaga and a girl called Vasilisa, who outwits the sorceress by using a magical doll to complete her impossible tasks.

FLESH-EATERS AND BLOOD-DRINKERS

Certain creatures strike terror into humans because we are their prey—they enjoy feeding on our bodies and drinking our blood. Many of these beings are undead, who have lived mortal lives, but live on after death in altered form.

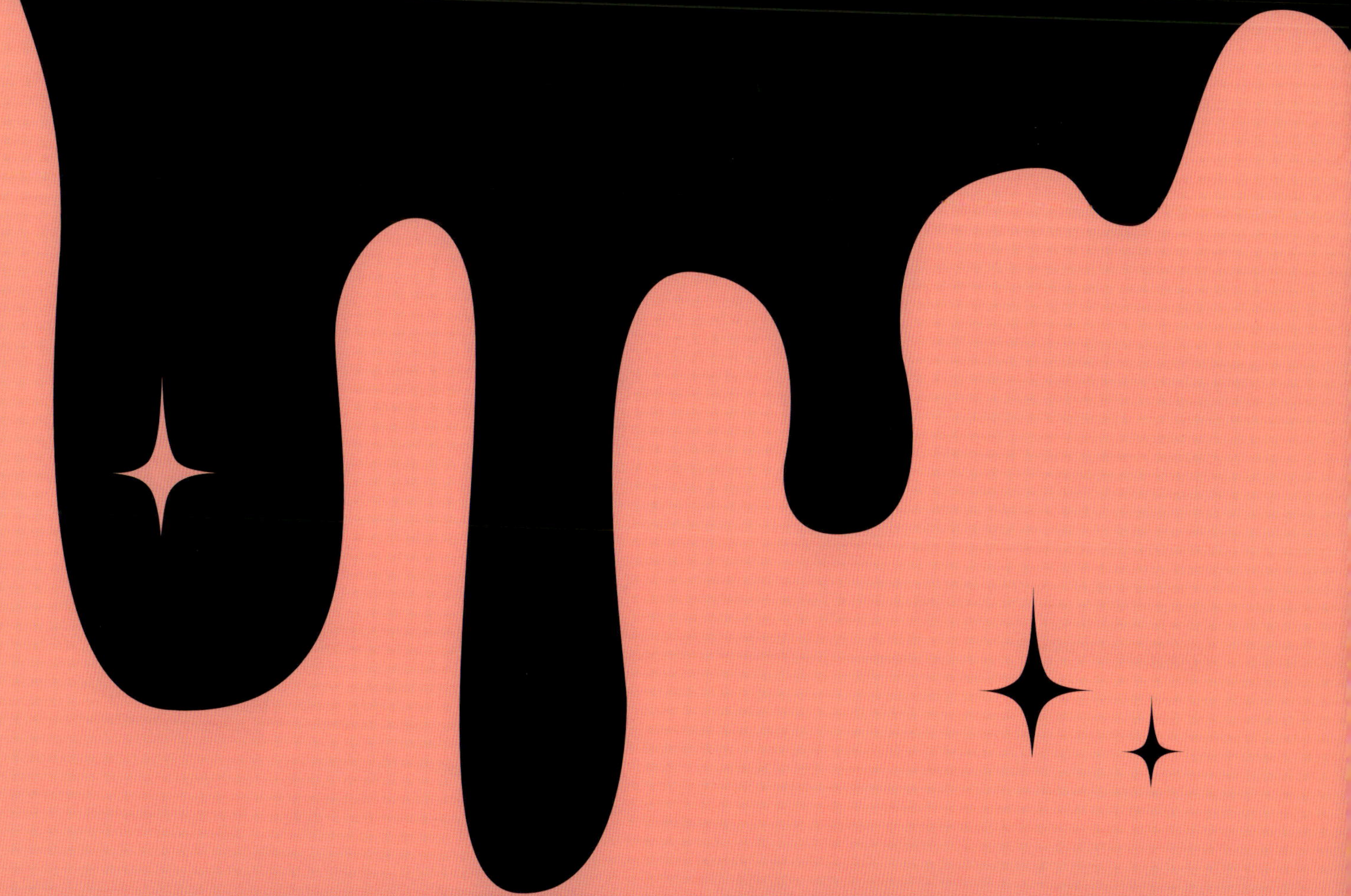

VAMPIRE

BLOODTHIRSTY PREDATOR

Long, pointed fangs are often a clue that an otherwise human-looking person might be a vampire. A vampire's fangs are key to its survival. It must use them to get its supply of food—human blood. Humans generally die after being bitten by a vampire, though there is also a risk that a bitten person might turn into a vampire themselves. These creatures appear in myths from around the world, in particular eastern Europe. They all drink blood, but some stories include other vampire abilities, such as shape-shifting into bats or mist.

This Polish painting from 1916 features a vampire that has taken the shape of a winged lizard.

VARIED VAMPIRES

Vampires appear in a huge range of stories, movies, and plays worldwide. Some look human, while others are spirit-like, monsterlike, or corpse-like. They might disguise themselves and live among us, or emerge from gloomy lairs only at night, to hunt for human prey.

The 19th-century British Varney novels feature a fanged monster cursed to become a vampire.

The German film Nosferatu was released in 1922, and features a vampire called Count Orlok.

The batlike betaal appear in Hindu beliefs.

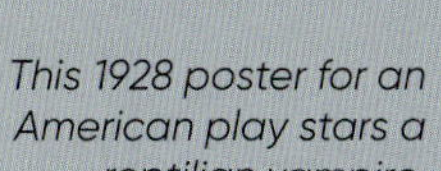

This 1928 poster for an American play stars a reptilian vampire.

"Better Than 'The Bat'"
N.Y. HERALD-TRIBUNE
DRACULA
THE WORLD FAMOUS
AMPIRE THRILLER

A 19th-century British drawing of a vampire sucking blood

DRACULA
6d.
BRAM STOKER
6d.
WESTMINSTER
Archibald Constable & Co Ltd
2 WHITEHALL GARDENS

Bram Stoker's 1897 novel Dracula features a vampire from Transylvania who can turn into a bat.

PUTTING ON A DEFENSE
Certain items are said to offer protection against vampires, such as garlic or crucifixes, holy water, and other religious symbols. But the only way to kill a vampire is to drive a wooden stake through its heart, cut off its head, and burn its remains.

Vampires have no reflection in a mirror.

A common vampire bat has fang-like front teeth.

FEASTING ON BLOOD
Vampires aren't the only sanguivores (creatures that feed on blood). They exist in nature, too. Vampire bats drink the blood of birds and large mammals. They use their fangs to bite into the flesh and make blood flow.

EERIE LIKENESS
Strzyga often look like owls. This clay carving of a strzyga with owllike features was made by Polish artist Dariusz Fluder.

Scaly, feathered ears frame this strzyga's face.

Two rows of long front teeth

Feathered body

STRZYGA
MURDEROUS MENACE

In Polish folklore, some women are born with two hearts and two souls. When they die, one heart stops beating and the other powers a bloodthirsty being known as the strzyga.
This vampire-like creature will remember her past life as a human and hunt down those who wronged her in life. The strzyga kills people, especially children, and then sucks out their blood. She can shapeshift into an owl. To make sure a strzyga could never leave her grave, people in medieval Europe burned her corpse face down, put a piece of flint under her tongue, and drove nails into her body.

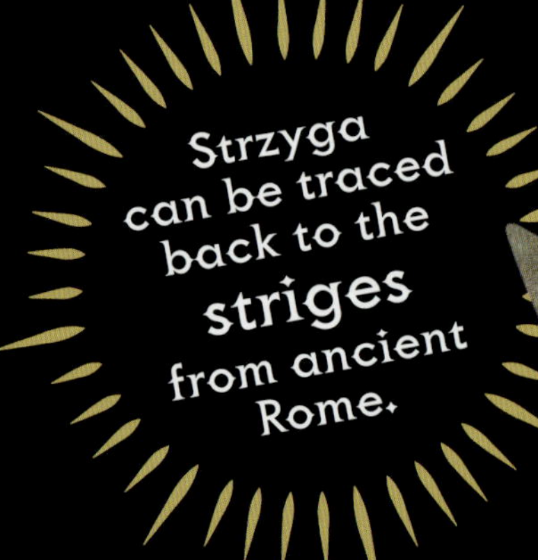

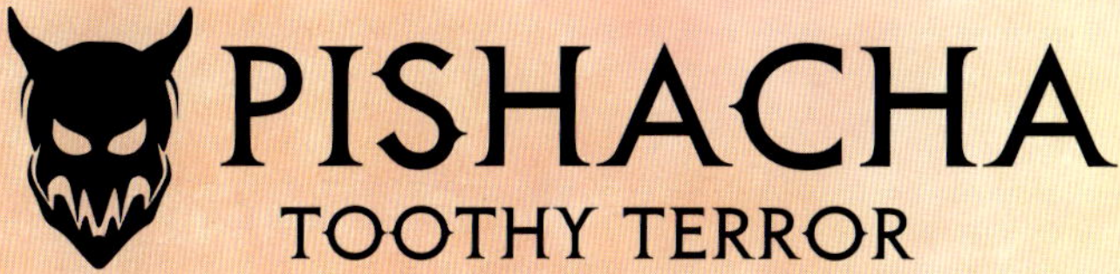

PISHACHA
TOOTHY TERROR

In Hindu beliefs, when a person dies an unnatural death, they are doomed to turn into a pishacha—a demonic being trapped between the realms of life and death. Pishachas spend their time in cremation grounds, feeding on the burned remains of dead people. They can possess people, and make them turn violent or insane. They can shape-shift into anything they want, and can hide themselves by turning invisible. Pishachas also cause disease and fever wherever they go, leaving a trail of death.

Pishachas come out at **dawn or dusk.**

These pishachas are ready to punish sinners in hell.

EVIL APPEARANCE
The powerful pishachas are hard to miss with their glaring eyes and vicious fangs, as seen in this wall painting in a cave at Sri Lanka's Aluvihare Rock Temple.

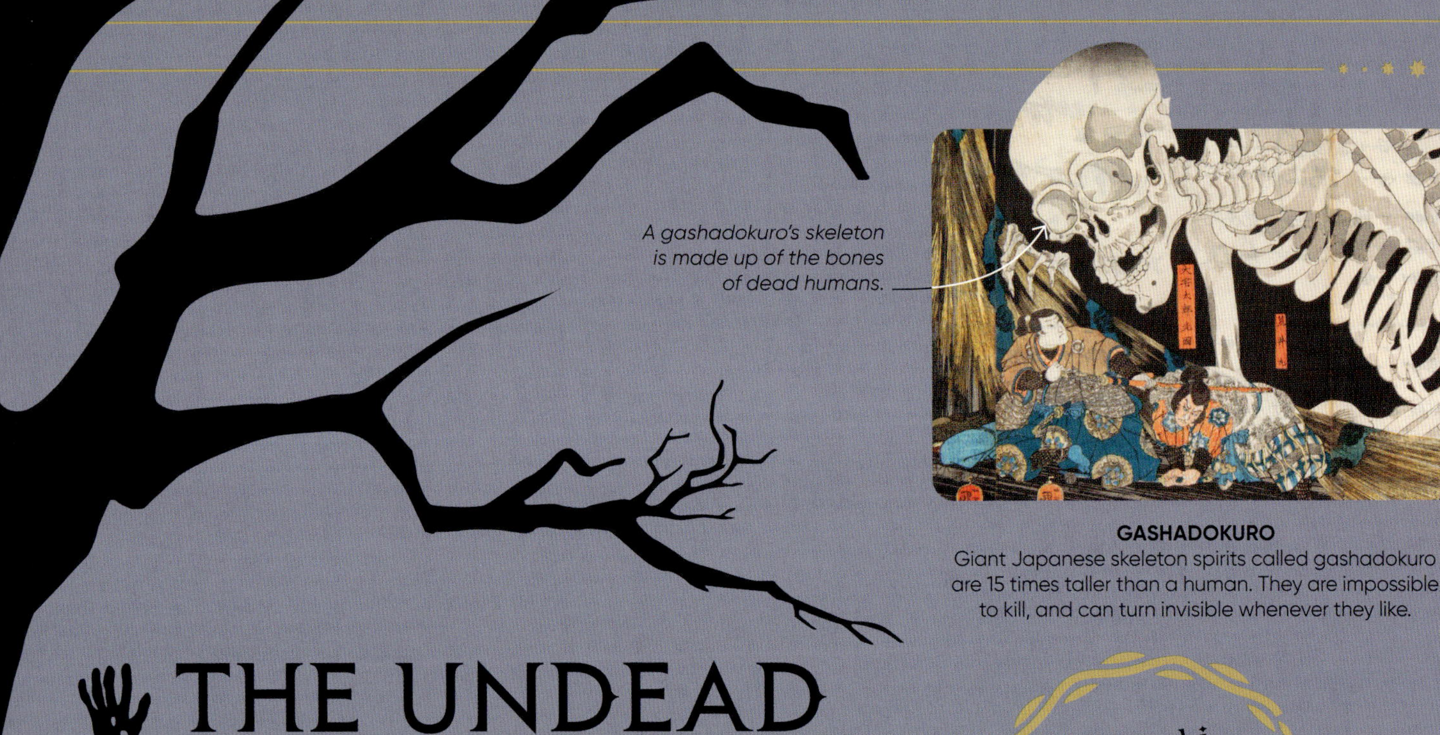

A gashadokuro's skeleton is made up of the bones of dead humans.

GASHADOKURO
Giant Japanese skeleton spirits called gashadokuro are 15 times taller than a human. They are impossible to kill, and can turn invisible whenever they like.

THE UNDEAD

UNREST AND DISORDER

Willingly or not, some creatures linger on once their mortal lives are over. They become part of a whole new class of beings—the undead.

Undead creatures have been reported from around the globe. They exist between life and the afterlife, returning in various forms after death. Some have physical forms, others are more ghostly. The undead generally wish ill upon the living, and some of them even eat the blood or flesh of those still alive. Take a look at some of the world's undead at your peril.

Jiangshi often feature in Chinese horror films.

This jiangshi has a long ponytail, called a queue.

Not even priests, nobles, or rich merchants are safe from revenants.

REVENANT
Deathly pale or gray, these undead are reanimated human corpses. Revenant is French for "returning." In Norse myths, they guard treasure in their graves, but they also roam among us, killing animals and people.

JIANGSHI
A jiangshi has long teeth and nails. This Chinese vampire is blind, and its corpse is stiff, so it hops along with its arms outstretched.

ZOMBIE
Originally from Africa and Haiti, a zombie is a human who has died and then been brought to life again. Zombies are brain-dead and their only aim is to find food, which could be you.

PRETA
In India, China, Japan, and Thailand these spirits are known as "hungry ghosts." They are eternally hungry, and seek out food that they can never swallow, due to their narrow throats.

DRAUGR
It is best not to disturb Scandinavian graves, in case you disturb a draugr—a revenant that is desperate to kill humans and reeks of decay.

AKAN PEOPLE
The Akan women in this photograph are performing a traditional dance. From the 12th century onward, the Akan people grew wealthy by clearing forests to mine for gold. Their culture is rich in mythology, too, including tales of many spirits and gods.

Mouth filled with sharp teeth

Sasabonsam toys with its prey before it attacks.

TREETOP HUNTER
The Sasabonsam usually hunts by hiding in a tree, waiting patiently to ambush prey passing by. Descriptions of it may vary, though it is usually said to have a human face, a long beard, teeth of iron, horns, and batlike wings—much like this 20th-century wooden carving of the creature by Ghanaian sculptor Osei Bonsu.

TRICKY THURSDAYS
In Akan culture, people do not enter the forest on Thursdays, which gives the land a chance to replenish itself. If you do go into the forest, beware: the Sasabonsam preys on those who flout the rules.

SASABONSAM
FOREST GUARDIAN

Lurking in the forests of West Africa is a bloodsucking monster with an eye for ecology.
The Sasabonsam, or Asanbosam, is a vampire-like creature found in the folklore of the Akan people, who live in Ghana, Togo, and the Ivory Coast. It hides in treetops, and sucks the blood of those who enter the forest when they should not. Missing hunters and farmers are often assumed to have become victims of the creature.

Hook-shaped feet allow the Sasabonsam to hang upside-down from trees.

WENDIGO

ENDLESS EATER

Tall and bone-thin, wendigos (or windigos) are wretchedly hungry no matter how much they have eaten. Wendigos wander the earth hunting for their next meal—of human flesh. They frequently appear in the stories of the Algonquian-speaking peoples in North America, such as the Cree, Ojibwe, and Blackfeet nations. Ever ravenous, wendigos are associated with winter and famine. Descriptions vary—they are sometimes fearsome, humanlike beasts, and sometimes ghostlike spirits that can possess human bodies. Every wendigo was once a human who turned into a cannibal—its bite turns its victims into cannibals, too, feeding on human flesh to survive.

Long, matted hair

Horns, sometimes antlers

BEYOND HUMAN
Wendigos are said to be much taller than humans, with glowing eyes, darting tongues, sharp claws, hearts of ice, and the stench of rotting flesh. This 20th-century portrait was created by Canadian First Nations artist Norval Morrisseau.

A person may turn into a wendigo if they are greedy.

Vultures wait for scraps from the next victim.

CANNIBALISM
If food is short, especially in harsh conditions, many animals become cannibals, and eat others of their own species. Even people have been known to become cannibals. Cannibalism is a common theme in myths from all over the world.

AUSTRALIA 45c

1994

A BUNYIP OF ABORIGINAL LEGEND

WATER MONSTER
The bunyip features in the traditional stories of the First Nations peoples of present-day Australia, and inspired this stamp issued in 1994.

BUNYIP
SWAMP CHOMPER

When in Australia, don't walk too close to dark lagoons, dank swamps, or murky pools. Lurking in the waters may be a deadly monster called the bunyip, waiting to pounce on you.

Some picture books show the bunyip as a harmless plant eater, but don't be fooled. This amphibious beast has a taste for humans, and ventures out of its watery lair when hungry. Described as either scaly or shaggy, it may have black and brown fur; an emu- or doglike head; and a broad, squat body like an alligator, with long claws. Just as scary are the blood-curdling roars it makes while on the prowl.

REAL OR HOAX
Pranksters and fraudsters have long tried to dupe the public by faking new evidence of mythological creatures. This bunyip skull, "discovered" in 1846, turned out to be the head of a deformed horse.

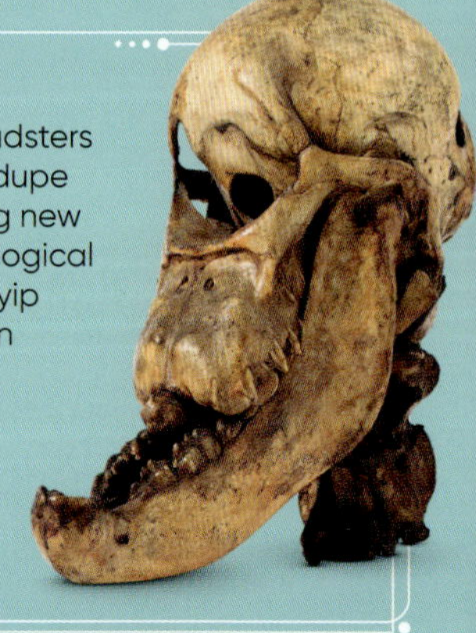

CHUPACABRA
CATTLE KILLER

Latin America's bloodsucking chupacabra has leathery skin, deadly fangs, and glowing red eyes. The first sightings of this creature were in Puerto Rico in the 1990s, most notably in 1995, when eight dead sheep were discovered drained of blood from two or three puncture wounds in the chest. Earlier livestock deaths in 1975 had also featured a total loss of blood, and were now linked to the same culprit. Since the 1990s, the chupacabra has roamed far and wide, with further sightings reported across Central, South, and North America.

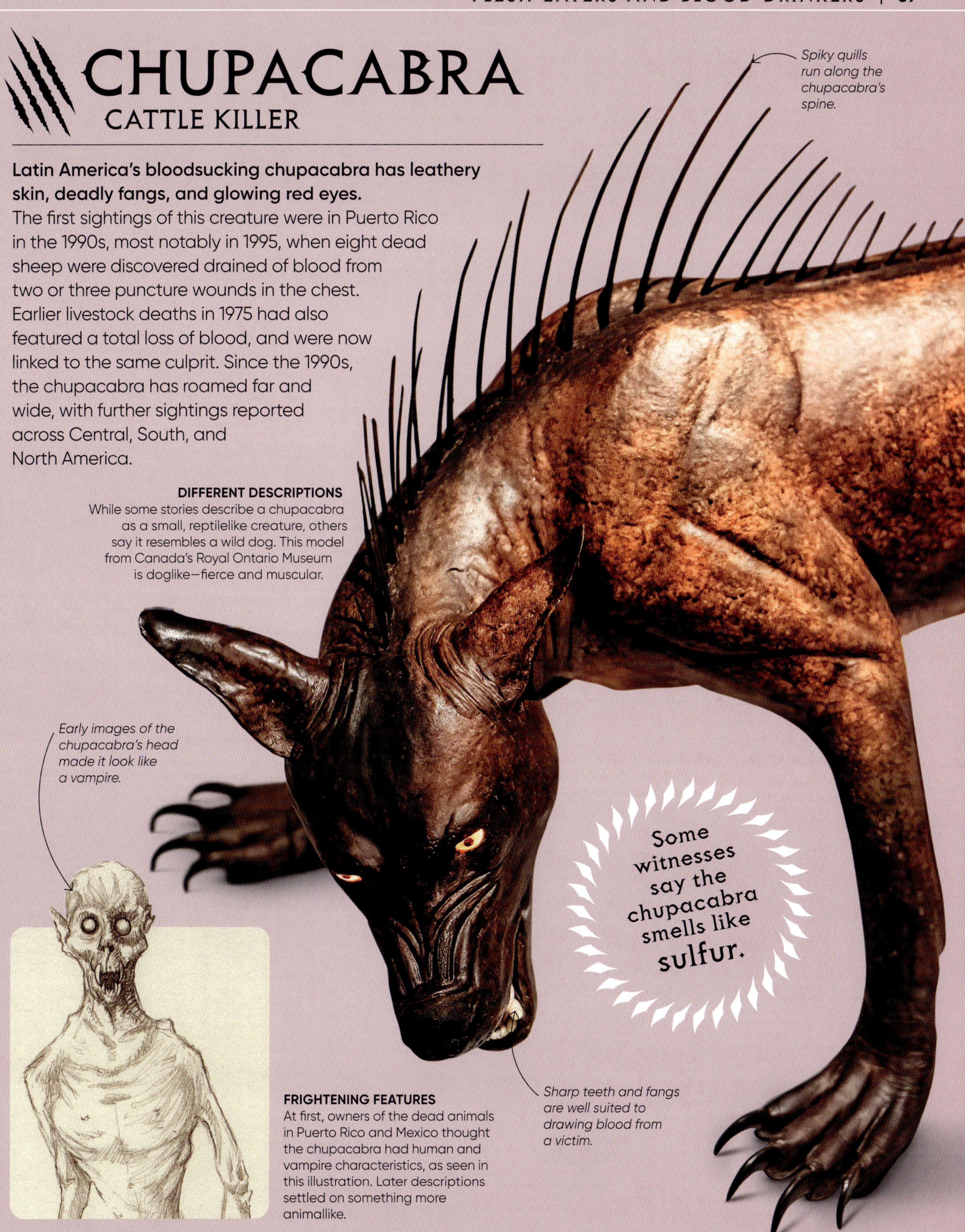

Spiky quills run along the chupacabra's spine.

DIFFERENT DESCRIPTIONS
While some stories describe a chupacabra as a small, reptilelike creature, others say it resembles a wild dog. This model from Canada's Royal Ontario Museum is doglike—fierce and muscular.

Early images of the chupacabra's head made it look like a vampire.

Some witnesses say the chupacabra smells like sulfur.

Sharp teeth and fangs are well suited to drawing blood from a victim.

FRIGHTENING FEATURES
At first, owners of the dead animals in Puerto Rico and Mexico thought the chupacabra had human and vampire characteristics, as seen in this illustration. Later descriptions settled on something more animallike.

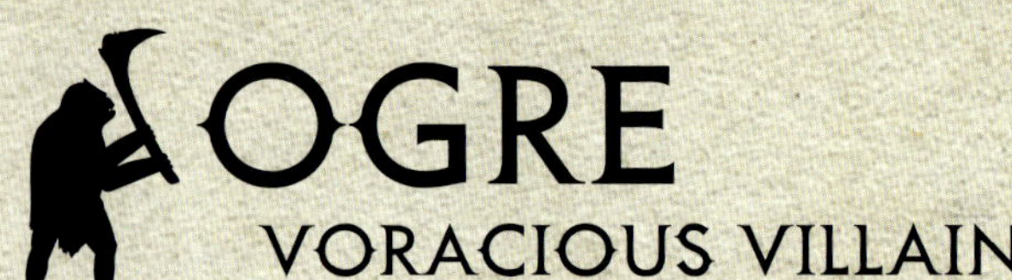

OGRE
VORACIOUS VILLAIN

Hide now if you've seen a huge, hairy, hideous beast with a ravenous appetite for people, especially babies and children. That's an ogre. Ogres make their presence known in caves, swamps, and forests all over the world, but they are particularly famous in Europe. The 17th-century fairy tales *Puss in Boots* and *Hop-o'-My-Thumb* by French author Charles Perrault feature ogres as villains that the hero overcomes with trickery and smart thinking. Folklore sometimes shows these dangerous monsters as shy or slow-witted giants.

THE MOUTH OF ORCUS
A stone ogre called Orcus greets visitors in the gardens at Bomarzo Monster Park near Rome, Italy. Orcus was a Roman god of the underworld who punished oath breakers. The Italian word *orco* later referred to people-eating monsters, as did the French word *ogre*.

BEWARE GRÝLA
The Icelandic ogress Grýla is known for cooking mischievous children in a large pot. In the 19th century, she became associated with Christmas, emerging during the holidays to steal naughty children.

STRIKING A DEAL
Ogres are generally not helpful, but in a story from Andrew Lang's *The Grey Fairy Book*, illustrated by Henry Justice Ford in 1905, an ogre agrees to let a boy named Antonio work for him for wages.

Ogres use clubs and spikes to clobber their victims.

Ogres are ill-tempered, and often **fight each other.**

Ogres often live in caves, which smell awful once they take up residence.

Antonio is not scared, and greets the ogre confidently.

IN THE SKIES

Wings come in useful for lots of creatures, including supernatural ones. For better or worse, the beings on these pages all have the ability to take to the air. Some of them have scaly wings; others have feathers; and one, the Firebird, is wreathed in flames.

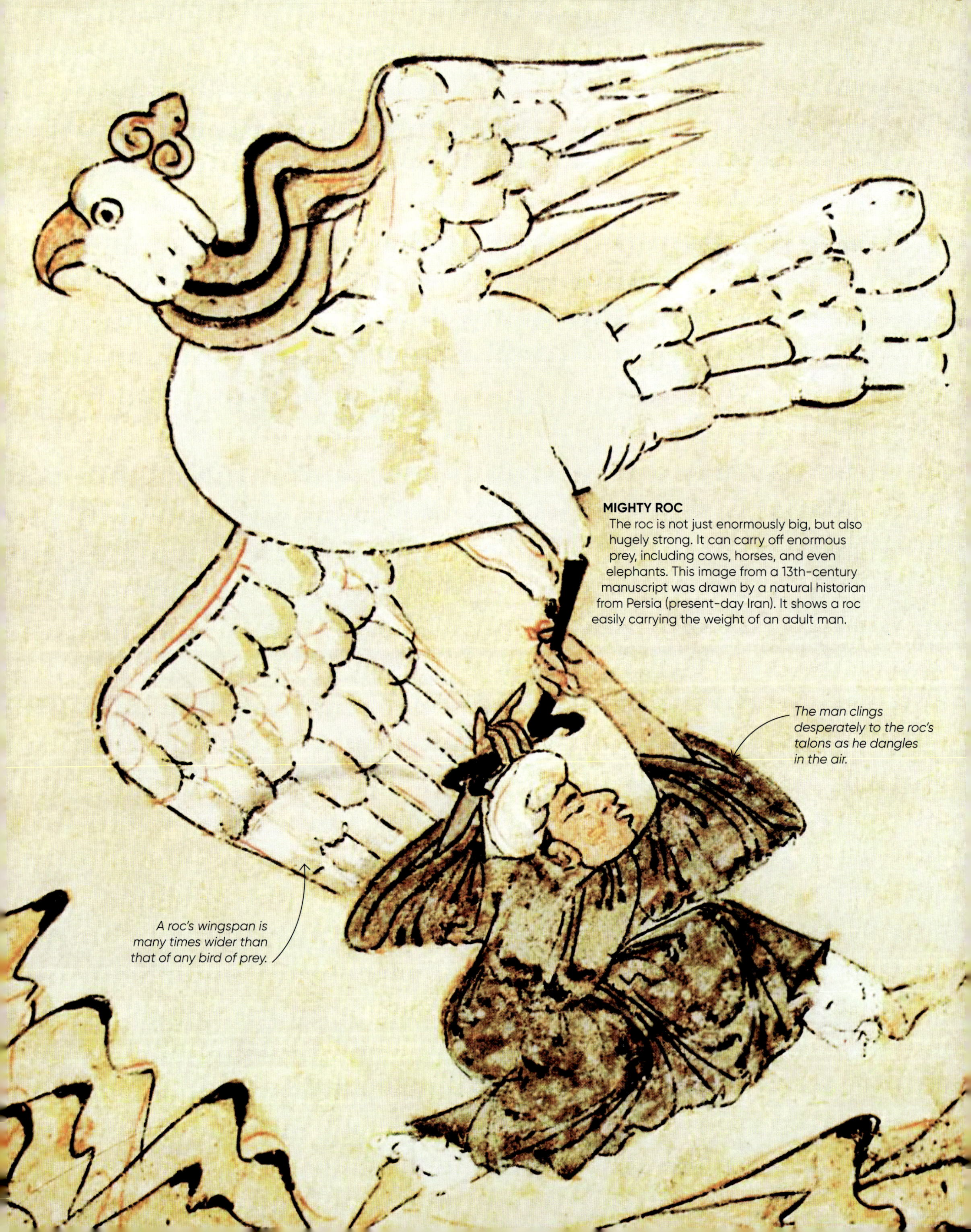

MIGHTY ROC
The roc is not just enormously big, but also hugely strong. It can carry off enormous prey, including cows, horses, and even elephants. This image from a 13th-century manuscript was drawn by a natural historian from Persia (present-day Iran). It shows a roc easily carrying the weight of an adult man.

The man clings desperately to the roc's talons as he dangles in the air.

A roc's wingspan is many times wider than that of any bird of prey.

The roc is so big, it can block out the sun.

The roc's egg is the size of a large boulder.

The sailors bind the chick's beak to subdue it.

GIANT EGG
In one story, Sinbad the Sailor and his crew came across a huge egg lying on a beach. They smashed open the egg and ate the chick that was growing inside it, earning them the wrath of the parent roc.

ROC
FLYING FIEND

Even the fiercest birds of prey would look tame next to the colossal, ferocious roc. A roc (or rukh) looks like an enormous eagle, with razor-sharp talons and beak. Anyone who damages a roc's egg or chick is in extreme danger, and should keep a careful eye on the skies in case the vengeful parent appears. While the origins of this creature are unclear, it features prominently in Arabic folk art and stories, including the collection of tales called *One Thousand and One Nights*. One man in these stories, Sinbad the Sailor, was unlucky enough to encounter a roc twice.

WORLD TRAVELER
Italian merchant Marco Polo traveled the world in the 13th century, and claimed to have seen a roc in eastern Africa. Here Marco Polo can be seen traveling with others in an illustration from the 14th-century world map called the Catalan Atlas.

RAVEN
WINGED SAVIOR

This cunning, shape-shifting bird is a hero because he shared light with the world.
Raven tricked his way into the Sky Chief's house, and used the light to create the sun, moon, and stars. Once Raven released the light, it flooded out into the world, ending the darkness. He appears in many Indigenous stories from North America, including those of the Tsimshian, Cherokee, Haida, and Tlingit peoples. They say that Raven discovered humanity itself.

MYTH TO OBJECT
Raven appears in the art and objects of many Indigenous peoples. He carries the light he stole in an object in his beak in this rattle. Among the Haida people, a chief or a shaman (priest) might use a rattle like this one in traditional ceremonies.

THUNDERBIRD
STORM BRINGER

With wings wide enough to stir up the wind and a beak that flashes bolts of lightning, the Thunderbird is a sight to behold. The Thunderbird's flight can create storms, with rain clouds rolling off his wings, accompanied by the sound of rumbling thunder. Thunderbird appears in the beliefs and stories of Indigenous peoples from North America, including those of the Arapaho, Ojibwe, Lakota, and Dakota peoples. The details of Thunderbird's story change from place to place, but he is always a powerful bird, associated with thunder, lightning, and water.

INSCRIBED ON PETROGLYPHS
Across North America, Indigenous peoples have created rock carvings called petroglyphs. These show stars, people, nature, and even mythological creatures. The Thunderbird appears often, as in this ancient petroglyph at the Legend Rock State Petroglyph Site in Wyoming.

MIGHTY SAVIOR
Once the Quillayute people were so desperate for food that they prayed to the Great Spirit for help. Thunderbird appeared in the sky, bringing them an entire whale for a meal, as seen in this image from the 19th century.

The whale fought hard to escape, but Thunderbird won eventually.

PHOENIX
IMMORTAL ICON

The glorious phoenix never dies—it is immortal, living forever in an endless cycle of fiery rebirth. An adult phoenix is at least the same size as an eagle, and each of its lives can last for hundreds of years. Phoenixes sing beautifully each morning, so their song accompanies the sun as it rises into the sky. They are able to heal with a single touch, and are seen as a symbol of hope. Phoenixes appear in myths from a wide range of places, including ancient Greece, Egypt, Persia (present-day Iran), and China.

Inherkhau was a worker who lived during the reigns of Pharaohs Ramses III and Ramses IV.

ANCIENT ORIGINS
The ancient Egyptian bird deity Bennu is shown in the tomb of Inherkhau in Luxor, Egypt. Bennu was linked to the sun, creation, and rebirth, and may have inspired stories of the phoenix in ancient Greek mythology.

FROM ASHES TO LIFE
When a phoenix reaches the end of its life, it builds itself a nest and burns up in a fiery blaze. A young phoenix chick emerges from its ashes, ready to live again, as seen in this image from a 12th-century English manuscript.

CELESTIAL HYBRID
A spectacular bird in this temple carving, the Fenghuang is also described as a hybrid of birds and other animals. It has celestial connections: the creature's eyes, head, back, wings, feet, and tail correspond to the sun, sky, the moon, wind, Earth, and planets.

ANCIENT SYMBOL
The *Shanhaijing* ("The Classic of Mountains nd Seas") was written in ancient China between the 3rd century BCE and 1st century CE. In this collection of stories about mythical beasts and laces, the Fenghuang (top left) was described

FENGHUANG
NOBLE BIRD

This bird is a symbol of all things good, including love, virtue, harmony, and grace.

A Fenghuang appears to humans very rarely, and a sighting has a particular meaning: a new emperor will soon be taking the throne of China. Fenghuang are often shown alongside Chinese dragons, which are a symbol of the Chinese emperors. They sing beautifully,

FEEDING ZAL
The Simurgh returns to its nest with food for her fledglings and a white-haired boy named Zal. He was abandoned at birth by his father, King Saam of Persia, and reared by the Simurgh. This spectacular scene of the bird's mountaintop nest was painted by Persian artist Abdul Aziz in about 1525.

SIMURGH
PLUMED PROTECTOR

Beautiful feathered tail

This spectacular winged creature was the protector of the mighty Persian Empire (centered in present-day Iran). The Simurgh is a gigantic winged messenger that flies between the heavens and Earth, and purifies the land and the waters where people live. This mystical bird with its long tail is big enough to carry off an elephant or a whale for dinner, and so old that it is said to have seen the world destroyed three times over. Originally from ancient Persia (present-day Iran), it also became famous in neighboring Armenia, Georgia, and Byzantium, which was the Eastern Roman Empire.

A MIRACLE OF BIRTH
Zal was given three magic tail feathers by the Simurgh, and returned home to become a great warrior-king. He married Rudaba, the princess of Kabul. When she went into labor, Zal summoned the Simurgh, who was skilled in medicine and taught him how to deliver the baby.

Rudaba watches her maid cradle the newborn Rustam, who will be a great hero.

The Simurgh chats with Zal.

The Simurgh is a formidable hunter but hates **snakes.**

Mosaic shows two Simurgh carrying white deer as they fly toward the sun.

ARTISTIC MOTIF
The Simurgh features in the dazzling mosaics that decorate the Nadir Divan-Begi madrasa, or Islamic center of learning, in Bukhara, Uzbekistan. Simurgh motifs in art symbolized wisdom and hope.

GOLDEN LOOT
The Firebird flees with an apple in this scene from the book *The Fairytale of Ivan Tsarevich, the Firebird, and the Gray Wolf*. Legend has it that the Firebird stole golden apples from the garden of the czar, Russia's emperor, to feed the poor.

FIREBIRD
BIRD OF LIGHT

Shining bright in Russian and other Slavic folklore in Central and Eastern Europe is the brilliant Firebird. This magical bird glows with the power of a thousand lights, its magnificent plumage glittering and gleaming like gold, and its eyes sparkling like shimmering crystals. The Firebird's song can cure the sick and help the blind to see. Attempts to capture the bird may end in blessings or lead to eternal doom.

Prince Ivan, illustrated by Russian artist Ivan Yakovlevich Bilibin

PRINCELY PURSUIT
Many fairy tales about the Firebird feature Ivan Tsarevich, son of the czar, and his attempts to capture the bird. He stayed up all night to get his chance, but when the time came to catch it, he only managed to pluck a single feather from its tail before it made its escape.

BASAN

FIERY FOWL

A ghostly birdlike being emerges only under the cover of darkness high in the Ehime mountains on the Japanese island of Shikoku. This is the turkey-sized basan, which can breathe fire from its mouth. By day, the basan would be easy to spot with its red crest and flame-colored feathers. But this elusive bird is nocturnal and avoids contact with humans. It feeds on the remnants of bonfires, protects forests, and brings good luck to those who respect nature.

FIRE ROOSTER
Sightings of this avian yōkai (monster) are extremely rare, but Japanese artist Takehara Shunsensai vividly shows the basan breathing fire like a dragon in this illustration from a book published in 1841. However, this is purely ghost fire—it produces no heat.

The basan is named after the sound of its flapping wings.

A bamboo grove is a likely home for a basan.

PEGASUS
WINGED WONDER

Pegasus was a magical and majestic winged beast soaring through the skies in the myths of ancient Greece. Blessed with extraordinary supernatural powers, this pure white stallion had huge, feathery wings and a gleaming, golden bridle. He was a loyal and brave workhorse who carried lightning bolts for the Olympian god Zeus. At the end of his life, Pegasus was rewarded with a permanent place in the heavens, gaining immortality as a starry constellation that still bears his name today.

Pegasus's father was Poseidon, god of horses.

Some Romans called the Muses Pegasides, in honor of the mythical horse.

SPRING TO LIFE
Wherever the galloping hooves of Pegasus touched the ground, great springs of water burst forth, including the Hippocrene Fountain. This was a sacred spot for the Muses—nine sisters who were water nymphs celebrated for personifying and inspiring the arts.

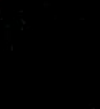

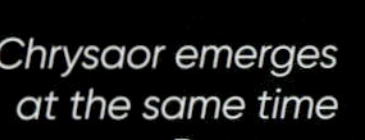

Pegasus is born fully grown.

Chrysaor emerges at the same time as Pegasus.

Medusa had wings, just like Pegasus.

BATTLE BORN
When the hero Perseus chopped off the gorgon Medusa's snake-haired head, two beings were born from her. The emergence of the brothers Pegasus and Chrysaor is captured in this limestone sculpture from the 5th century BCE.

FLYING STEED
Winged horses star in mythologies and beliefs around the world. Hindu sacred texts feature a white, winged horse, named Devadatta, who takes flight for his master Kalki, an avatar of the supreme God Vishnu.

Bellerophon brandishes a spear as he flies on the back of Pegasus.

KILLING CHIMERA
The Greek hero Bellerophon managed to tame the wild Pegasus using a special golden bridle. The horse carried him into battle to slay the fire-breathing, three-headed Chimera, depicted in this ancient Roman stone and glass mosaic from the 2nd century CE.

Chimera had the heads of a lion and a goat, and a serpent for a tail.

SIREN
BIRDLIKE TEMPTRESS

When it comes to sirens, don't believe everything you see! They may look beautiful but their intentions are usually deadly.
The sirens sit on stony shores, singing and playing music to entice ships. As the vessels come closer to hear them, they are smashed on the rocks, killing everyone on board. The sirens' song is so attractive that none who hear it are able to resist their call. These murderous musicians of ancient Greek epics have bodies that are part bird and part human.

Sirens are companions of **Persephone**, queen of the underworld.

Odysseus stands spellbound but unable to move.

BIRDLIKE FEATURES
The earliest stories about sirens describe them as almost entirely bird, with the faces and voices of women, as seen on the interior (left) of this drinking cup from the 6th century BCE. Later stories feature sirens that look like women, but with only the wings and feet of a bird.

Siren at top of ancient Greek stela (grave marker)

A SONG FOR THE DEAD
The ancient Greeks often used figures of sirens to decorate monuments to the dead. The sirens were shown playing musical instruments, or singing sad songs to mourn people who had died.

This ancient Roman mosaic from 101–300 CE shows a siren playing a lyre.

STEERING CLEAR
The sirens first appear in Homer's *Odyssey*, written in about the 8th century BCE. The hero Odysseus makes his crew plug their ears with wax and tie him to the mast, so he can hear the sirens but cannot jump into the sea as his ship sails past.

BENEATH THE WAVES

Our streams, rivers, ponds, lakes, and seas are home to a wide range of supernatural beings. Water provides a useful hiding place and a rich hunting ground. Some supernatural creatures spend their whole lives underwater, others occasionally find their way onto land.

HYDRA
MANY-HEADED MONSTER

Deep in the swampy marshes of Lerna in ancient Greece lurked a massive, multiheaded monster named the Hydra. Taking its name from the Greek word for water, the Hydra was the terrifying offspring of Typhon, the father of all monsters, and a female serpent hybrid named Echidna, the mother of all monsters. In Greek mythology, the Hydra is variously depicted as an evil serpent and a devilish dragon. Either way, the Hydra's foul breath and poisonous blood was said to pollute all the water in the area. The creature was virtually invincible, thanks to its extraordinary regenerative powers—as soon as one of its heads was chopped off, two more grew back in its place.

Mighty Hercules wears the skin of a huge lion he killed.

Some say the Hydra had **hundreds of heads!**

REGENERATION IN NATURE
An aquatic invertebrate called the green hydra shares the same regenerative abilities as the mythical monster Hydra. It can reproduce by forming a bud on its body that eventually falls off as it grows into a new hydra.

HEROIC HERCULES
The legendary Greek hero Hercules (sometimes called Heracles) battles the Hydra in this 16th-century Italian Renaissance rock crystal plaque. Hercules was given 12 near-impossible labors, or tasks, by King Eurystheus, and killing the Hydra was only the second one. As Hercules cut off each head, his nephew Iolaus quickly scorched the neck stumps with fire to stop any more heads from growing.

JÖRMUNGANDR

MIDGARD SERPENT

This snake is large enough to wrap himself all the way around the world and grasp his tail in his mouth. Jörmungandr appears in Norse myths. When he was young, the gods heard a prophecy that he and his siblings would cause trouble, and had them banished or imprisoned. Jörmungandr was sent to the bottom of the sea that encircles Midgard, the human world.

Midgard, the human realm, is at the center of Yggdrasil.

WORLD TREE
The nine realms in the Norse cosmos—which housed gods, humans, supernatural beings, and the dead—are all located in different parts of Yggdrasil, the World Tree. Wrapped around its roots is another serpent called Níðhöggr.

THE FINAL BATTLE
Norse myths feature Ragnarök—a colossal battle at the end of the world. Part of the prophecy about Ragnarök includes a fight between Jörmungandr and Thor, god of thunder, which will leave both of them dead. The conflict is depicted in this painting from 1905 by German artist Emil Doepler.

Jörmungandr is a child of the trickster god Loki.

SCYLLA
SAILORS' DOOM

Perched high on a cliff over a tricky stretch of water is Scylla, a terrifying sea monster with six heads. Sail too slowly past Scylla and she might gobble you up—any ship that ventures near her is in mortal danger. Scylla appears in three of the ancient Greek epic poems, including Homer's *Odyssey*. The legendary heroes Jason and Odysseus both sailed close to her cliff instead of risking another danger nearby—the whirlpool Charybdis.

Each of Scylla's heads snatches its own meal.

DEADLY CHOICE
Across the water from Scylla is Charybdis, a huge whirlpool that sucks ships down into the depths. To pass, ships' captains had to choose which obstacle they would face, risking death either way.

Scylla was a beautiful **nymph** who was cursed by the gods.

Charybdis drinks in and belches out seawater, forming a whirlpool.

LEVIATHAN

PRIMORDIAL MONSTER

How many sea creatures can make a whale look small?
The Leviathan can. One version of this beast in the Bible is a dragonlike monster that embodies chaos and evil. It has a reptilian head and spiny ridges on its back and tail, and it causes havoc as it plows through the ocean. It may have been inspired by the ancient Mesopotamian tale of a similar serpent named Yamm. Like the Norse Jörmungandr (see page 112), this immense creature is a sign of the Apocalypse to come at the end of the world.

WHAT IS THE APOCALYPSE?
Many mythologies and religions around the world share the idea that a cataclysmic event will bring about the end of everything. The Apocalypse in the Bible will amount to a total destruction of the world. This scene from the 11th-century manuscript *Beatus de León* shows animals and beheaded sinners tumble into the waters above the serpent Leviathan.

OCEAN MARAUDER
In the 19th century, French artist Gustave Doré illustrated this seagoing nightmare among his many engravings of scenes from the Bible. Here, the Leviathan thrashes around in the sea, turning the waters into a tumultuous mix of waves and foam.

The name **Leviathan** comes from an ancient Hebrew word meaning "coiled."

VANQUISHING THE WORM
John Lambton is in danger in John D. Batten's illustration from *More English Fairy Tales*, published in 1894. The worm tried to crush Lambton, but injured itself on his armor's spikes, before Lambton chopped it into pieces.

LAMBTON WORM
TWISTED MENACE

England's County Durham in the 13th century is the setting for this story. One day, young John Lambton skipped church to go fishing, but all he caught was an ugly worm with a salamander-like head. It didn't look edible, so John threw it down an old well. Little did he know that this worm would soon grow into a terrifying serpent slithering around the countryside, feeding on livestock and children. Although John slayed it eventually, his family remained cursed for generations, each member meeting a horrible death.

The worm could drink **20 gallons** (76 liters) of milk in a day.

KRAKEN

TENTACLED TITAN

Truly the stuff of nightmares, this ancient Scandinavian sea monster strikes fear in the hearts of sailors from Norway to Greenland. Among the largest mythical creatures ever, the Kraken is a gigantic octopus that appears from nowhere and terrorizes ships without warning. If the Kraken fails to take down a ship with its colossal tentacles, it creates a treacherous, swirling whirlpool to drag the vessel underwater. In 1830, the monster came to life in English poet Alfred, Lord Tennyson's sonnet *The Kraken*, which described this terrifying titan in alarming detail.

CLASSIFYING THE KRAKEN
In 1753, the Norwegian bishop Erik Pontoppidan popularized the Kraken by including it among other living creatures in his book *First Attempt at Norway's Natural History*. He had heard fishermen describe the Kraken as an enormous monster, as big as an island, with arms so long it could pull down a large ship.

The Kraken may use its **poop** to lure fish.

ANIMAL ORIGINS
The Kraken can be traced back to Norse sagas. A 13th-century Norse text described a creature called the Hafgufa as enormous. In 1753, this gigantic beast—now called the Kraken—was described as having tentacles. It may have been based on the giant squid, the world's biggest invertebrate, which can grow up to 50 ft (15 m).

No ship is strong enough to survive the Kraken.

OUT OF THE DEPTHS
The true scale of the Kraken is captured in this dramatic illustration originally made in 1887. Stormy weather is said to be the trigger for this mighty monster to emerge from the deepest depths and launch an attack. It hunts submarines, too, as Captain Nemo found in the 1870 novel *Twenty Thousand Leagues Under the Sea*.

Many sightings of Champ refer to his long neck.

Onlookers recoil in horror at the sight of Champ.

EYEWITNESS ACCOUNTS
Champ looks like a giant serpent in most news stories, as in this 1886 scene from the *Illustrated Police News*. In the late 1970s, a photograph reportedly showing the creature's head sticking out from the water sparked a lot of debate. But the photo could not be authenticated and has since been debunked.

Some people think Champ is probably a garfish.

CHAMP
UNDERWATER TERROR

Vermont is famous for maple syrup, fall colors—and the creature lurking in the depths of Lake Champlain. Iroquois stories describe an enormous horned serpent named Onyare'kowa in this lake. Nicknamed Champ (or Champy), it has been sighted more than 300 times over the years. While many people claim to have seen a creature that looks like a prehistoric reptile, some eyewitnesses have reported spotting a horselike or doglike head on a long, scaly body.

Champ is the official mascot for the Vermont Lake Monsters.

FROM MYTH TO MASCOT
Sports teams are sometimes known to adopt mythical mascots, from the Chunichi Dragons baseball team in Japan to the Vermont Lake Monsters baseball team in the US.

MOKELE MBEMBE

RIVERINE REPTILE

Have any prehistoric dinosaurs actually survived? Some people believe the Mokele Mbembe of Central Africa has done just that. This fiercely territorial beast is highly protective of its home in the Congo River Basin, and will destroy any watercraft that get too close for comfort. It is the size of an elephant, with a smooth, brownish-gray skin, a long and flexible neck, and a powerful tail like that of an alligator. Cryptozoologists and dinosaur hunters led many expeditions to find evidence of this creature's existence in the 20th century, but the Mokele Mbembe has evaded capture to this day.

Ogopogo features in this public art display in Kelowna, Canada.

LAKE GUARDIANS
Stories of monsters in lakes are as old as human settlements nearby. The water-dwelling serpent Ogopogo lives in Canada's Okanagan Lake, and features prominently in the stories of the Okanagan and Secwépemc peoples of present-day British Columbia. This serpent is an evil entity and demands a sacrifice to allow safe passage through the water.

Mokele Mbembe means "one who stops the flow of water."

The curved head makes the creature resemble some dinosaurs that fed in shallow water.

Spikes on the back are similar to the ones on some dinosaurs.

A FINE SPECIMEN
This wood carving of the Mokele Mbembe was made in Congo in the 1980s. It shows the beast with a peaceful expression. The lack of teeth suggests it is a herbivore. Some sightings report a single long tooth like a rhinoceros horn.

LOCH NESS MONSTER

DWELLER IN THE DEEP

Hidden deep in the waters of Loch Ness in Scotland lurks a mysterious monster, fondly known as Nessie. A 6th-century Pictish carving of a strange serpentlike creature may be one of the earliest depictions of this legendary beast. Since then, Nessie has been "spotted" many times in Loch Ness. Eyewitness accounts range from a gigantic prehistoric reptile with large fins and a long neck to an enormous, eellike serpent. Many people wonder how a massive monster came to reside in Loch Ness in the first place. The loch is connected to the North Sea by a series of lochs and rivers, including the Ness River—perhaps a prehistoric monster once swam in this way, and has remained trapped in the loch ever since.

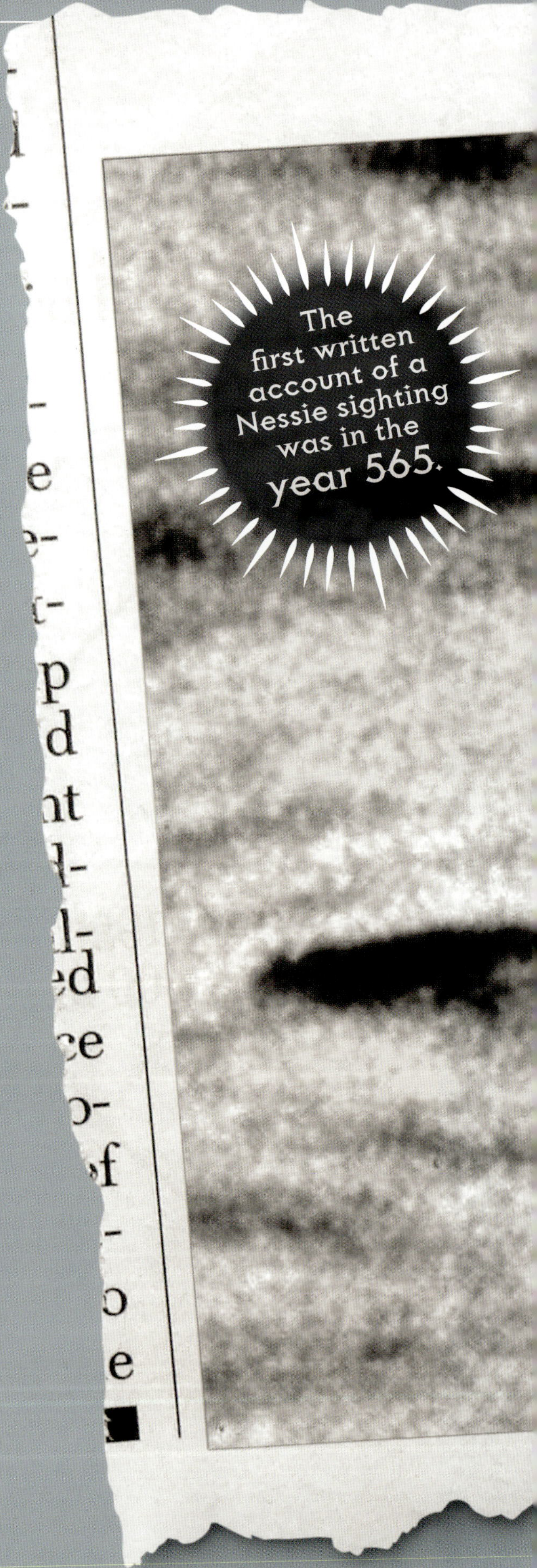

The first written account of a Nessie sighting was in the year 565.

HUNTING FOR NESSIE
People have searched for the Loch Ness Monster for centuries. The hunt continues today, using high-tech equipment such as drones, thermal cameras that can "see" body heat, and underwater microphones that can pick up the faintest sounds. This 2018 expedition from the University of Otago, New Zealand, took a different approach—they tested the waters of the loch for DNA in the skin, feathers, and poop left behind by the inhabitants of the lake.

PICTURING THE MONSTER
In 1933, an eyewitness account described Nessie as a huge, prehistoric animal. British zoologist Maurice Burton sent the report to several artists, asking them to draw Nessie. The drawings contradicted one another: one gave it a short neck and a doglike snout, while another gave it a long neck, reptilian nose, and backward-pointing ears.

CAUGHT ON CAMERA
In 1934, this photo of Nessie was published on the front page of a British newspaper, sparking a media frenzy about the monster's existence. To this day, it is the most famous photo of Nessie, even though it was revealed to be a fake in 1994.

WARNING SIGNS
Visitors to the loch are greeted by these signs of Nessie, warning them to stay away from its waters. Loch Ness is 755 ft (230 m) deep, and bitterly cold throughout the year. Scientists say an animal of Nessie's size would need much deeper, warmer waters to survive.

ASPIDOCHELONE
COLOSSAL BEAST

An aspidochelone's back might offer a tempting break for sailors who have been at sea a long time, but light a fire at your peril. The creature is so massive that it can easily be mistaken for an island when it floats on the water's surface. Called aspidochelones by the ancient Greeks, these sea monsters appear in stories around the world, described as whales, vast sea turtles, or giant fish.

The aspidochelone gives off a sweet smell to lure fish.

The men cry out in terror.

The ship sinks as the sailors try to escape.

MONSTROUS FISH
In medieval Europe, an illustrated bestiary (book of beasts) was bound to include an aspidochelone. In this scene from a French bestiary made around 1270, it is a giant fish. The beast dives for deeper waters after sailors mistake it for an island and light a cooking fire on its back.

Umibōzu are linked to giant waves and tsunamis.

CHANGING APPEARANCE
Accounts vary, but most descriptions of the umibōzu include a pair of enormous eyes. This one, which looks like a catfish with long red feelers, appears in a Japanese scroll from the 17th century.

Only the head of the umibōzu is seen above the waves in this Japanese illustration from the 1850s.

UMIBŌZU
SHIP WRECKER

From a calm sea rises a strange creature with deadly intentions. As an umibōzu emerges, the water begins to heave, swiftly turning tumultuous and deadly to those who sail upon it. In Japanese tales, this yōkai (monster) may lunge at a ship, demand a bucket or barrel, then use it to swamp the ship with water, drowning everyone on board. Sailors can trick it by giving it a bottomless bucket, which can never be filled.

SEA MONKS
Classical Japanese literature often pictures umibōzu with dark, humanlike features as they rise up out of the sea. They are described as having smooth, shaven heads, which give them their name "umibōzu"—meaning "sea monk."

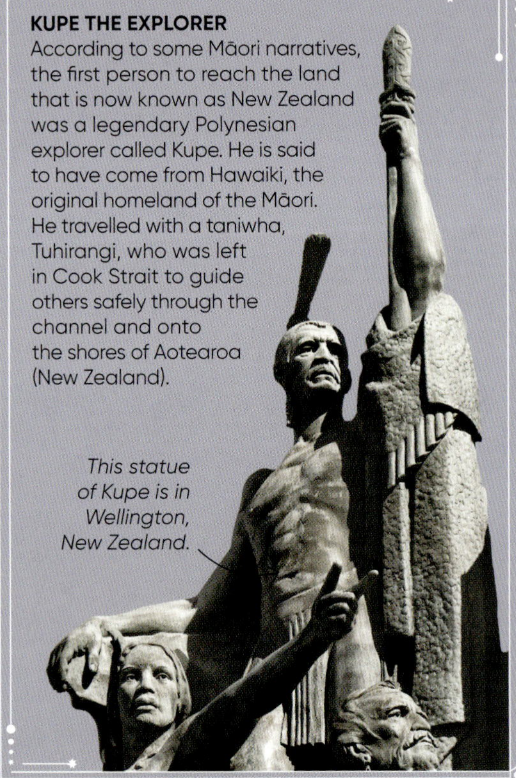

KUPE THE EXPLORER
According to some Māori narratives, the first person to reach the land that is now known as New Zealand was a legendary Polynesian explorer called Kupe. He is said to have come from Hawaiki, the original homeland of the Māori. He travelled with a taniwha, Tuhirangi, who was left in Cook Strait to guide others safely through the channel and onto the shores of Aotearoa (New Zealand).

This statue of Kupe is in Wellington, New Zealand.

SHIFTING FORM
Taniwha are shape-shifters that can take the form of whales, sharks, or even inanimate objects, such as logs. Some within the Māori community describe them as resembling dragons, serpents, or giant lizards with scaly, reptilian bodies, long, sharp claws, and even wings—as shown in this postage stamp from 1960. It was inspired by a famous piece of ancient Māori rock art called the Ōpihi taniwha, discovered in a cave above the Ōpihi River in Te Waipounamu (New Zealand's South Island).

TANIWHA
SUPER SERPENT

In the waters of New Zealand live long, dragonlike taniwha. These huge creatures prefer the watery places where few humans go, such as deep pools, remote caves, and dangerous currents and breakers at sea. They have two very different roles in Māori folklore. They are protectors of tribes, who leave them offerings, but they can also be hostile, kidnapping people and even eating them.

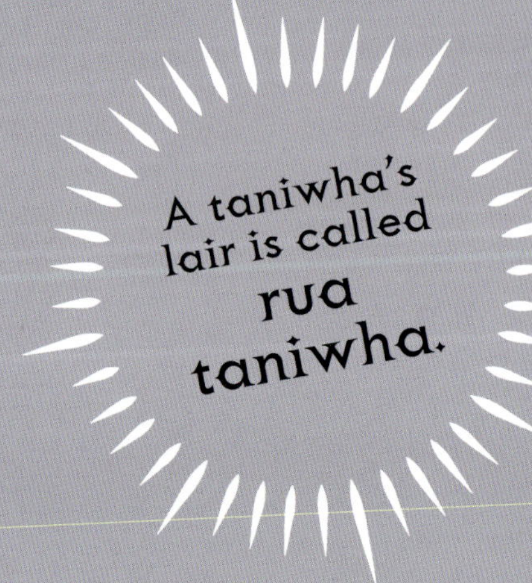

TIDDALIK
THIRSTY CROAKER

Some First Nations Australian creation stories describe how a frog called Tiddalik swallowed every single drop of water. Without water, the land cracked and dried, and plants struggled to survive, creating a dire situation for all the other animals. The details of this story vary across the First Nations Australian peoples, but there is always a thirsty frog at the heart of it. Much of present-day Australia is desertlike, but these stories explain it may not have always been that way.

ORIGIN OF DROUGHT
In First Nations Australian beliefs, stories featuring animals and sacred beings are often used to teach people about natural disasters. By drinking all the water, Tiddalik created drought in Australia. This story may have originated among the Gunai people, the traditional custodians of most of present-day Gippsland in southeastern Australia.

RELEASING THE WATERS
The animals tried everything they could think of to make Tiddalik release the water. Eventually, they made him laugh, and the water flowed back out of him. This painting of Tiddalik laughing is by First Nations Australian artist Karen Lee Mungarrja.

Tiddalik is surrounded by other animals.

USHI-ONI
COASTAL HUNTER

An idyllic stroll along the beach can turn into an arachnophobic nightmare in Japanese mythology. Lurking at the water's edge are the ushi-oni, whose name means "ox demon." These spiderlike monsters come armed with huge horns, crushing claws, and powerful jaws. Poison spews from their fangs as they lie in wait to attack unsuspecting people and gobble them down in an instant.

MYTHICAL GUARDIAN
Not all depictions of an ushi-oni are negative. In some parts of Japan, local fishermen consider the ushi-oni to be a guardian of the sea. Others believe it wards off evil spirits and brings prosperity. People in the city of Uwajima celebrate an annual ushi-oni festival, which features large puppets resembling the creature.

PARTNERS IN CRIME
Nure-onna, the snake woman of Nara, is another ancient Japanese terror, with a woman's head on a serpent's body. According to some myths, ushi-oni and Nure-onna often join forces to hunt, giving their victims no chance of survival.

If you look into an ushi-oni's eyes, it may drain your soul.

OX-HEADED SPIDER
This image comes from the *Bakemono no e*, a late 17th-century Japanese "monster" scroll that illustrates 35 supernatural creatures. It shows a typical ushi-oni in all its grotesque glory. In some stories, an ushi-oni may have the head of an ox but wear human clothing, or fly through the air with the wings of an insect.

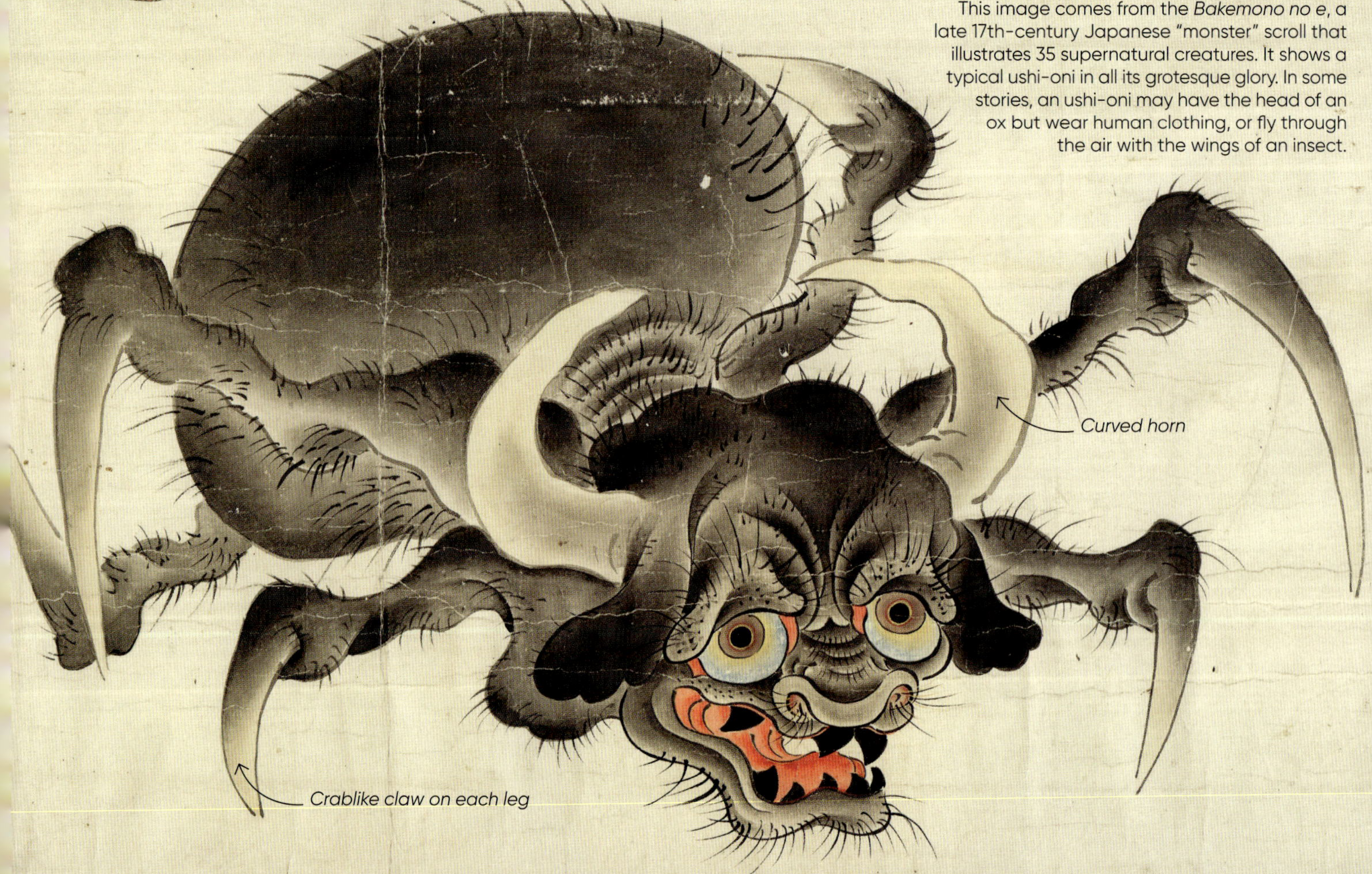

Curved horn

Crablike claw on each leg

Tail covered in fish scales

PROTECTIVE CARVINGS
A makara is a common motif found in Hindu and Buddhist temples across Asia. It was usually carved on entrances to temples and throne rooms, but it also appears on water spouts and gargoyles. This sandstone carving of a crocodile-headed makara was made in the 2nd century BCE in Madhya Pradesh, India.

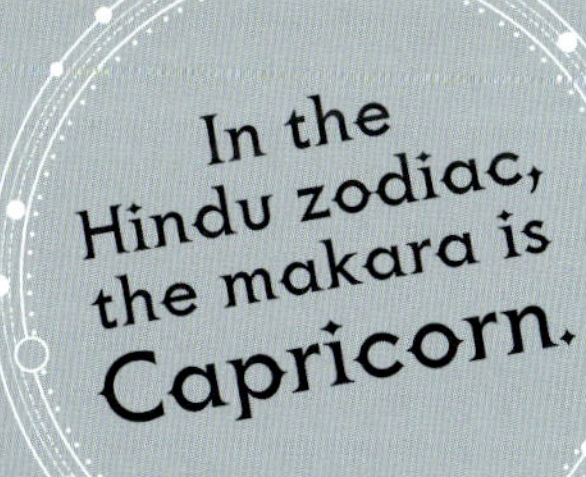

VESSEL OF VARUNA
The Hindu water god Varuna sails across the seas on the back of a makara in this 18th-century painting.

MAKARA
GATEWAY GUARDIAN

This powerful hybrid makes an appearance in many sacred stories from across Southeast Asia.
The makara have many forms, usually featuring the head of an elephant or deer and the body of an aquatic animal, such as a crocodile or fish. In Hindu and Buddhist stories, they play the role of gatekeeper, protecting sacred buildings, but they are also the transportation of choice for many Hindu deities.

KELPIE
SAVAGE SHAPE-SHIFTER

Beware a dark horse standing near a loch (lake) in Scotland. This is no ordinary horse, but a creature called a kelpie, which has appeared in Scottish and Irish folktales for hundreds of years. Many Celtic lakes and seas are associated with a kelpie. This shape-shifting creature, which can look like a man, lures its unsuspecting victims onto its back, and carries them off into deep waters to feed on them.

A prince is carried across a river by a glashtyn in an Irish folktale.

THE GLASHTYN
Similar to the kelpie is the glashtyn, a hairy goblin-like creature from the Isle of Man in the Irish Sea. When leaving the water, it takes the form of a horse, or even a horse-human hybrid. It likes to pursue women on land, and drag them into the sea.

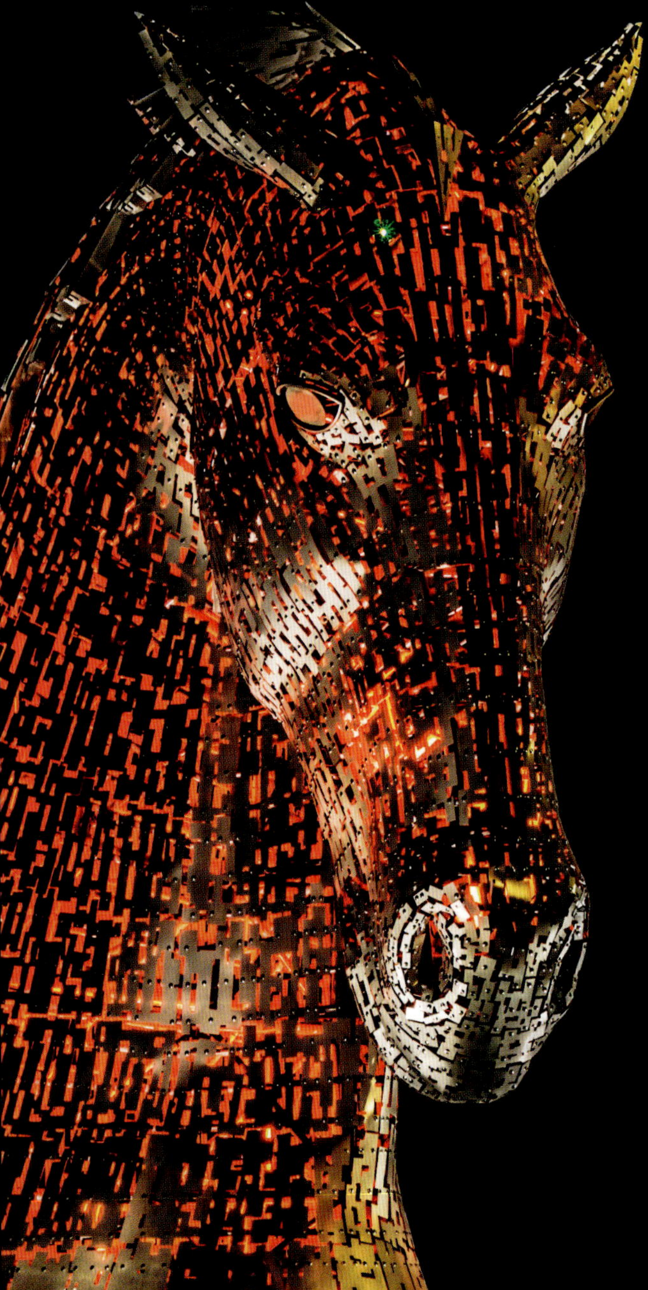

THE KELPIES
This pair of 98-ft- (30-m-) tall horsehead sculptures in Grangemouth, Scotland, is called *The Kelpies*. They are made of steel, and were installed in 2014. They are shown here lit up at night.

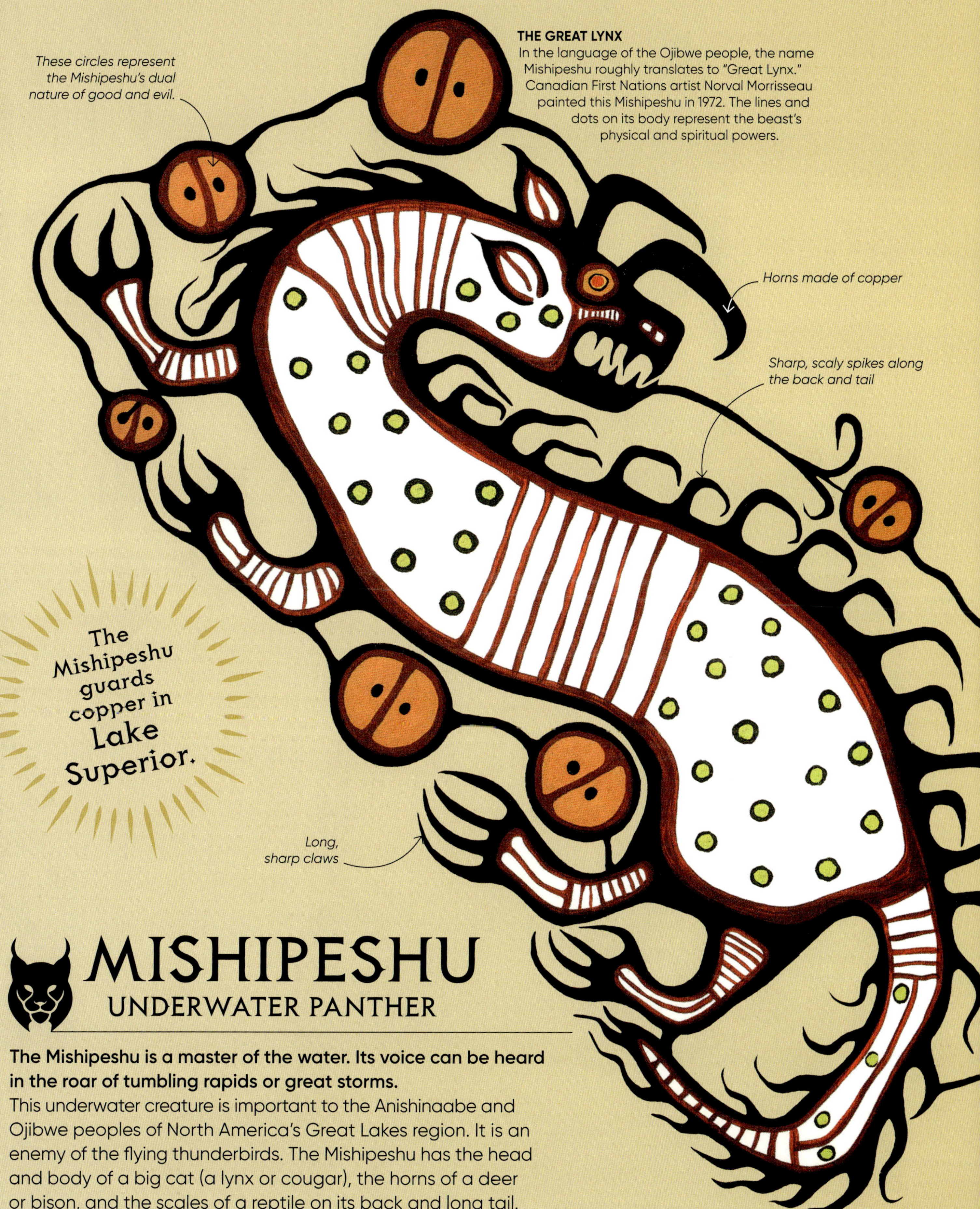

THE GREAT LYNX
In the language of the Ojibwe people, the name Mishipeshu roughly translates to "Great Lynx." Canadian First Nations artist Norval Morrisseau painted this Mishipeshu in 1972. The lines and dots on its body represent the beast's physical and spiritual powers.

MISHIPESHU

UNDERWATER PANTHER

The Mishipeshu is a master of the water. Its voice can be heard in the roar of tumbling rapids or great storms.
This underwater creature is important to the Anishinaabe and Ojibwe peoples of North America's Great Lakes region. It is an enemy of the flying thunderbirds. The Mishipeshu has the head and body of a big cat (a lynx or cougar), the horns of a deer or bison, and the scales of a reptile on its back and long tail.

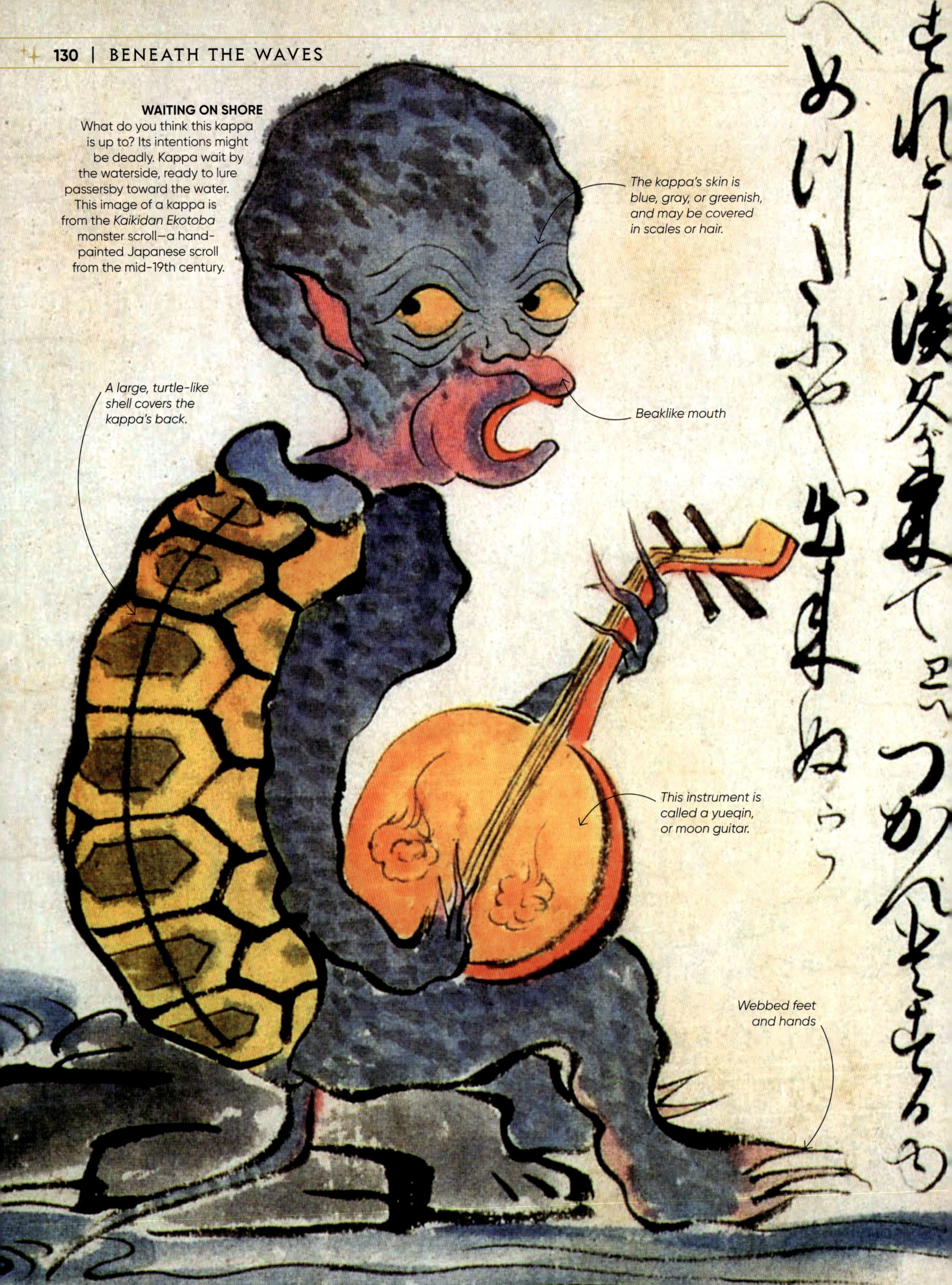

WAITING ON SHORE
What do you think this kappa is up to? Its intentions might be deadly. Kappa wait by the waterside, ready to lure passersby toward the water. This image of a kappa is from the *Kaikidan Ekotoba* monster scroll—a hand-painted Japanese scroll from the mid-19th century.

KAPPA
TERRIBLE TURTLE

Beware! Japan's waters may not be as safe as they look. It is said that kappa lurk beneath them. They are violent, child-size yōkai (monsters) with turtle shells.

Kappa spend their lives in and around rivers, and are always on the lookout for people to drag down into the depths. Many stories describe a dish-like cavity on top of each kappa's head, which contains a strange liquid—the creature's life force. If you come face to face with a kappa, try to trick it into nodding or shaking its head—if the liquid is spilled, it will be severely weakened. These reptilian yōkai have added watery terror to Japanese folk stories since at least the 17th century.

The writing says "it is scary around here."

WARNING SIGNS
This poster from the Japanese city of Saitama uses a kappa to symbolize danger. In parts of Japan, these posters warn children who might be tempted to play near a river.

Human head

Turtle's shell

MYTHICAL TURTLES
Turtles and turtle-like creatures appear in myths from all over the world. In Japanese mythology, another turtle-yōkai is the minogame—a creature that can live for 10,000 years. Elsewhere in Asia, turtles appear in stories from places such as Persia (present-day Iran) and India. This picture of a human-headed turtle is from a 17th-century manuscript from Mughal India.

Dish-like cavity to hold life force

CUCUMBER CRAZY
The kappa enjoys melons, eggplant, and pumpkins, but its favorite food is cucumbers. People sometimes leave cucumbers as offerings, trying to bribe the kappa into leaving them alone. Sogenji Temple in Tokyo, Japan, is dedicated to the kappa—many stone statues of kappa dot the temple grounds. The temple also houses an object said to be a kappa's mummified arm.

AMAZING HYBRIDS

The creatures in this chapter have mixed-up bodies, made of a little bit of this and a little bit of that. Parts of them look like real-life animals, but shuffled together to make something completely new and extra powerful.

SPHINX
GREAT GUARDIAN

The ancient and powerful sphinx has roots in different mythologies. Ancient Egyptian stories feature a strange hybrid guardian with the body of a lion but the head of a human or ram (male sheep). The pharaohs who ruled Egypt built huge sphinx statues to guard their tombs and temples. In ancient Greece, writers described a terrifying monster with the face of a woman, the body of a lion, and the wings of a bird. This version of the sphinx still guarded tombs but was also famous for posing riddles with near-impossible answers.

This sphinx statue was carved out of a massive block of limestone.

PROTECTING THE PYRAMIDS
The Great Sphinx at Giza is the largest of the sphinx statues in Egypt. It guards the tombs and pyramids in the Giza pyramid complex, and faces eastwards to greet the rising Sun. The statue has the body of a lion and a human face, and was built around 2500 BCE. The faces of sphinx statues were often modeled on those of the ruling pharaoh.

TEMPLE RELIC
Granite was used to make this beautifully carved sphinx statue, which comes from the temple of the female pharaoh Hatshepsut near the city of Luxor, Egypt. Its face resembles the pharaoh. The combination of a lion's body and the queen's head symbolized power, with lions standing for strength and royalty.

RIDDLE OF THE SPHINX
An ancient Greek legend describes a meeting between the sphinx and a Greek prince called Oedipus. The sphinx had been eating passersby who could not solve its riddle, but Oedipus knew the answer, making the creature so angry that it killed itself.

Egyptian sphinxes are often seen wearing a pharaoh's headdress, called a nemes.

Oedipus becomes the first and only person to solve the riddle.

SHAN DANCE
In this traditional dance from Myanmar, each pair of performers dresses as a kinnara and a kinnari. They make birdlike movements to the beating of drums and gongs, opening and closing the wings on their costumes.

Kinnara lead very long lives.

Gold leaf covers the bronze statue.

Jewels adorn the body and swanlike tail.

KINNARA
HYBRID HELPER

You can rest assured that when you are in need, there will be kinnara watching over you. Kinnara are beautiful male fairies that hail from the forests of the Himalayas. They feature in Hinduism and Buddhism, with varying descriptions across Southeast Asia. In many places, they are depicted as half-human and half-bird or half-horse. They are highly skilled at music and poetry. A female kinnara is called a kinnari.

KINNERA
Kinnara and kinnari can be seen playing zithers (stringed tubelike instruments) in art. They share their name with the kinnera, a zither used in the folk songs of the Chenchu and Dakkali peoples of India's Deccan plateau. The sounds from the instrument's strings resonate with its bamboo tube and the hollowed-out gourds attached to it.

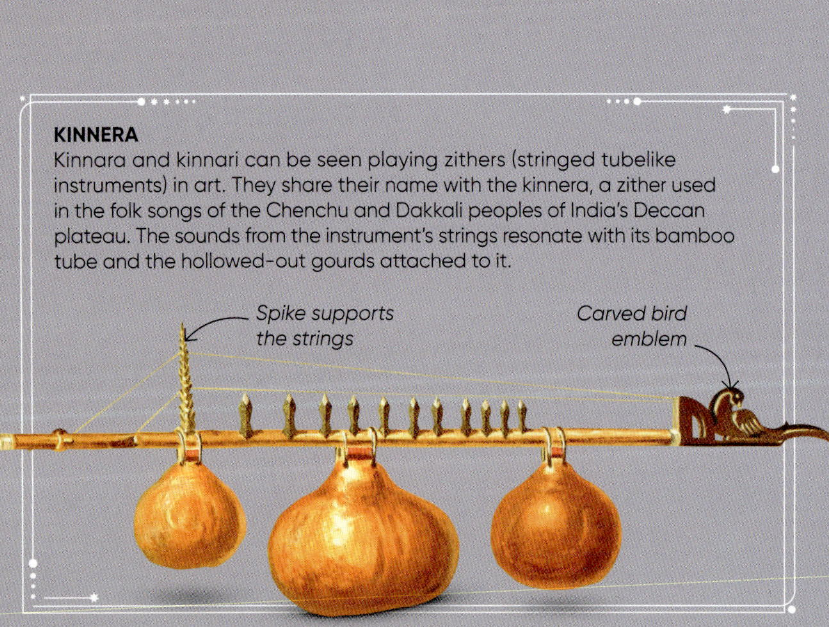

Spike supports the strings

Carved bird emblem

GOLDEN MINSTREL
This statue of a kinnara stands in Bangkok's Wat Phra Kaew ("Temple of the Emerald Buddha"), the most sacred Buddhist temple in Thailand. It has a man's head, arms, and torso, and a swan's legs, wings, and tail.

MANTICORE

MOTLEY BEAST

Three rows of teeth and sharp claws make the manticore an adept hunter in Central Asia and Europe.

This hybrid's name comes from the Farsi word for "man-eater." The manticore has a taste for human flesh, and can paralyze and swallow its victims whole. Anyone unfortunate enough to encounter this predator would be startled by its roar, which sounds like a fanfare of trumpets. The manticore may have originated in India or Persia (present-day Iran)—places that were visited by ancient Greek travelers, who then wrote about it.

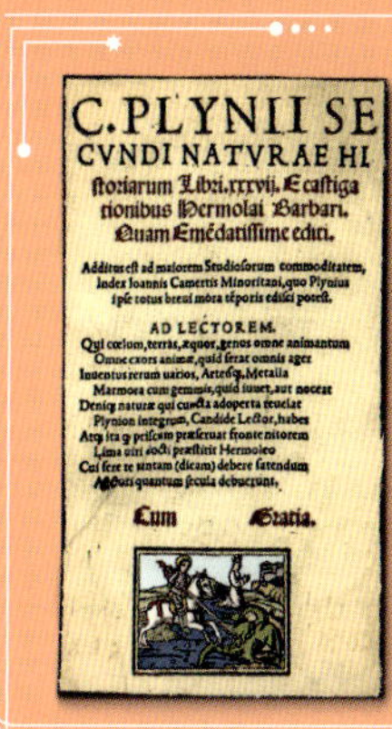

C.PLYNII SE
CVNDI NATVRAE HI
storiarum Libri.xxxvij. E castiga
tionibus Hermolai Barbari.
Quam Emēdatissime editi.

Additus est ad maiorem Studiosorum commoditatem,
Index Ioannis Camertis Minoritani, quo Plynius
ipse totus breui mora tēporis edisci potest.

AD LECTOREM.

Qui cœlum, terras, æquor, genus omne animantum
Omne exors animæ, quid ferat omnis ager
Inuentus rerum uarios, Artesq;, Metalla
Marmora cum gemmis, quid iuuet, aut noceat
Deniq; naturæ qui cuncta adoperta reuelat
Plynion integrum, Candide Lector, habes
Atq; ita q priscum præseruat fronte nitorem
Lima uiri docti præstitit Hermoleo
Cui fere te tantum (dicam) debere fatendum
Autori quantum secula debuerunt.

Cum Gratia.

MAKING IT REAL

Classical and medieval manuscripts often mistook mythical beings for real ones. In the 1st century CE, Pliny the Elder, a Roman author and naturalist, included the manticore in his book *Naturalis Historia*. Even this 1519 edition shows St. Michael and a dragon on its front page.

The manticore can shoot its tail spines like arrows.

MIGHTY MANTICORE

This regal manticore appears in a 13th-century bestiary from Rochester, UK. It is depicted with a human head, a lion's body, and a dragon's or scorpion's tail.

CENTAUR
HALF-HUMAN HALF-HORSE

Centaurs are wild hybrid horses that are human from the waist up and famed for both violence and learning.
First depicted some 3,000 years ago in Bronze Age pottery, centaurs can be found roaming through the forests and mountains of Thessaly, a region in Greece renowned for its horses and riders. They are important characters in ancient Greek myths, where they often fight—or teach—legendary heroes, including Hercules and Achilles. Most of the centaurs in these stories are male, but females do exist—they are called centaurides.

A centaur attacks a Lapith host.

BLOODY BATTLE
Alongside the centaurs lived a tribe of humans called the Lapiths. The centaurs were invited to a Lapith royal wedding, where they started a fight that became extremely bloody—the centaurs were almost annihilated. Known as the Centauromachy, this battle was portrayed as the triumph of civilization (the Lapiths) over barbarians (the centaurs).

NAMING CONSTELLATIONS
Many of the constellations we see in the night skies are named after mythical creatures, and two of them are centaurs. The lines in this picture captured over New Zealand trace the constellation Centaurus (in the middle)—this was also the name of a centaur who was the first to group stars into constellations. Another constellation named Sagittarius represents a centaur as an archer drawing his bow.

TRAINER OF HEROES
The wisest centaur in Greek mythology was Chiron. He tutored Achilles and other legendary heroes in medicine, music, riding, hunting, and bravery in battle. In this Roman fresco from Pompeii in Italy, Chiron teaches the young Achilles to play an instrument called the kithara, or lyre.

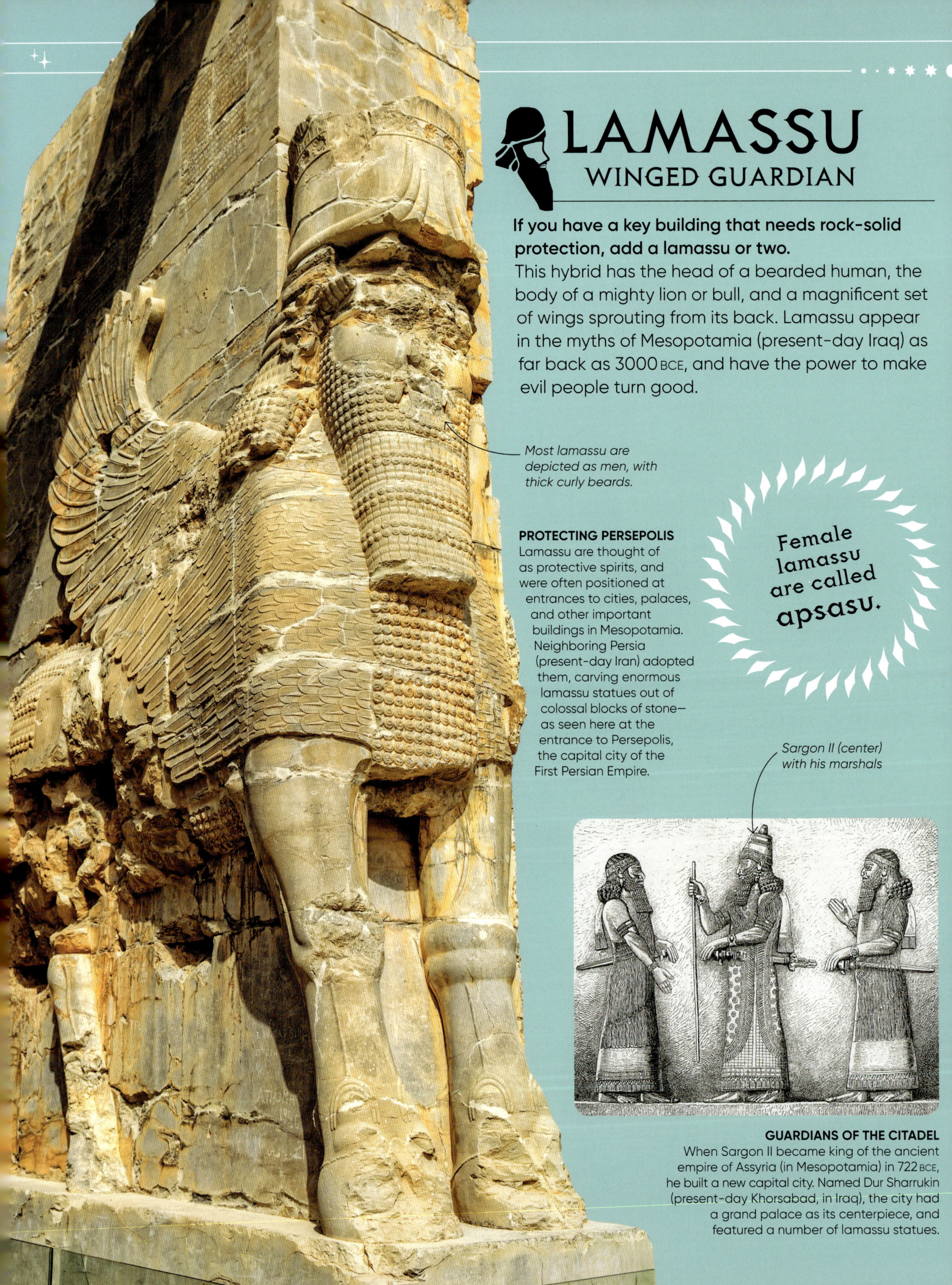

LAMASSU
WINGED GUARDIAN

If you have a key building that needs rock-solid protection, add a lamassu or two.
This hybrid has the head of a bearded human, the body of a mighty lion or bull, and a magnificent set of wings sprouting from its back. Lamassu appear in the myths of Mesopotamia (present-day Iraq) as far back as 3000 BCE, and have the power to make evil people turn good.

Most lamassu are depicted as men, with thick curly beards.

PROTECTING PERSEPOLIS
Lamassu are thought of as protective spirits, and were often positioned at entrances to cities, palaces, and other important buildings in Mesopotamia. Neighboring Persia (present-day Iran) adopted them, carving enormous lamassu statues out of colossal blocks of stone—as seen here at the entrance to Persepolis, the capital city of the First Persian Empire.

Female lamassu are called apsasu.

Sargon II (center) with his marshals

GUARDIANS OF THE CITADEL
When Sargon II became king of the ancient empire of Assyria (in Mesopotamia) in 722 BCE, he built a new capital city. Named Dur Sharrukin (present-day Khorsabad, in Iraq), the city had a grand palace as its centerpiece, and featured a number of lamassu statues.

MINOTAUR
MONSTROUS BULL

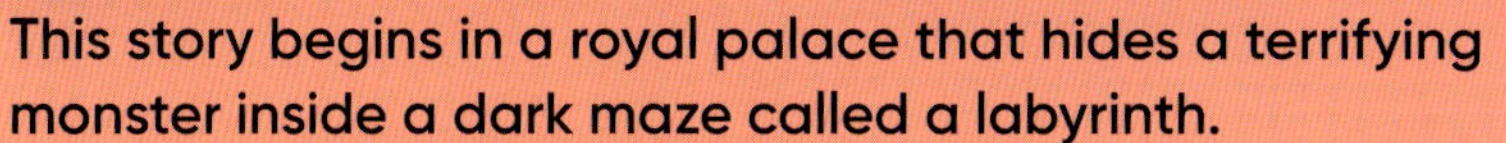

This story begins in a royal palace that hides a terrifying monster inside a dark maze called a labyrinth. The beast was called the Minotaur—it had a bull's head on a human body, and its food of choice was human flesh. Its labyrinth was designed to confuse, so that once a person had entered, escape was almost impossible. King Minos of Crete, ruler of the Minoans, kept the Minotaur imprisoned here, and would rid himself of enemies by feeding them to the beast.

BULL LEAPING
Bulls were sacred to the Minoans, and feature in their art. As shown in this fresco from the Palace of Knossos in Crete, athletes made daring leaps across a bull's back. Bull leaping may have been a popular ritual sport for the Minoans.

Theseus uses a sword given to him by his father, the King of Athens.

Legendary Greek inventor Daedalus designed the Minotaur's maze.

The Minotaur, although far stronger, falls to its knees upon defeat.

SLAYING THE MINOTAUR
The Minotaur was finally eliminated by the legendary Greek hero Theseus, who traveled to Crete determined to kill it. In one version of the story, he slayed the Minotaur using a sword, as shown in this black-figure pottery from ancient Greece, dating back to the 6th century BCE. In some other versions, Theseus used a club, or even his bare hands, to kill the beast.

EUROPEAN ART
A mermaid swims with her children in *Mermaids in the Deep*, a 19th-century painting by English painter Edward Burne-Jones. Mermaids became popular in European art and literature during the Renaissance (14th–16th centuries).

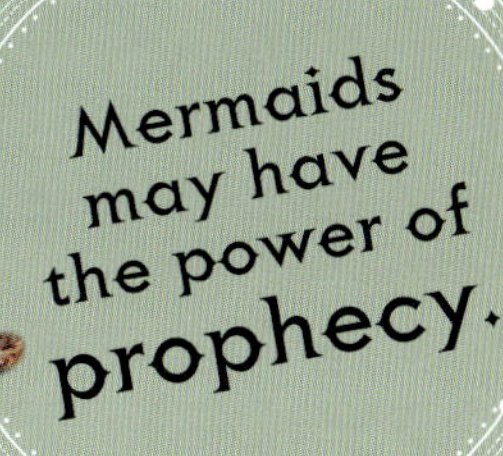

ORNATE FIGUREHEAD
From the 16th to the 20th centuries, wooden mermaids often decorated the prows of ships. Sailors believed that the figureheads would bring good luck and guide their ships safely home.

MERMAID
SEA MAIDEN

Mermaids are alluring creatures of the sea with captivating beauty and a melodious voice, but dive deeper and you'll discover a darker side.

These half-human, half-fish hybrids are notorious for drawing ships to their doom and imprisoning sailors in their murky underwater kingdom. The ghastly sirens of ancient Greece are sometimes shown as mermaids, but the earliest tales of mermaids come from ancient Syria, around 3,000 years ago. Ever since, spotting a mermaid has been an omen for storms, shipwrecks, and drowning at sea.

LITTLE MERMAID
Mermaids continued to be popular in European literature after the 16th century. Danish writer Hans Christian Andersen's story *Den lille havfrue* ("The Little Mermaid") was originally published in 1837 in a collection of fairy tales, and continues to be popular with children even today. It features a mermaid princess who wishes to be human—as seen in this illustration from 1913 by W. Heath Robinson.

This sculpture dates from around 100 CE.

SYRIAN ORIGIN
The first mermaid was Atargatis, the ancient Syrian goddess of fertility, who was worshipped around 1000 BCE. She threw herself into a lake after accidentally killing her human lover, but the waters transformed her into a mermaid.

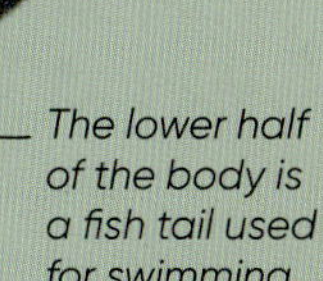

The lower half of the body is a fish tail used for swimming.

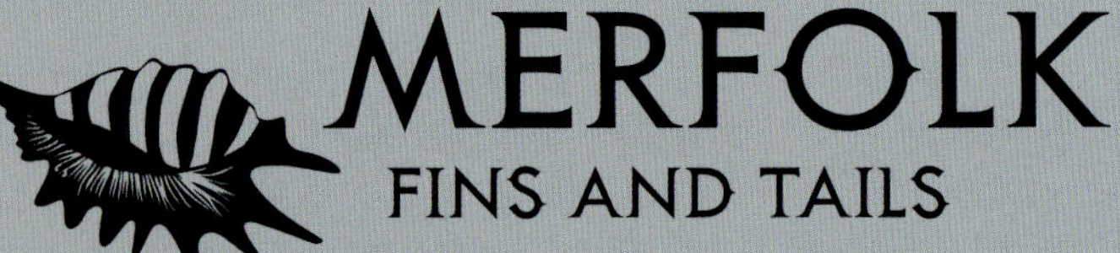

MERFOLK
FINS AND TAILS

Merpeople have been swimming in the seas for thousands of years. These half-human, half-fish creatures from around the world share one common trait: the upper part of their body is always human. Among merfolk, the mermaids are almost always beautiful, while their male counterparts, the mermen, can be hideous or handsome. But looks can be deceiving—some merfolk are friendly and helpful, others try their best to lure people to their deaths.

This 19th-century ningyo wears an elaborate headdress and robes.

MERROW
The Irish merrow is a classic mermaid, as seen in this 15th-century stone carving from Clonfert Cathedral in Ireland. They sometimes tempt human men to live with them under the sea, and male merrows are known to kidnap sailors.

GULNARE
In a story from *The Thousand and One Nights* (a collection of Western Asian folktales), Gulnare is a beautiful woman with a hidden past as a mermaid. She marries a Persian king, and has a son, who can live on land and under water.

NINGYO
Japanese merfolk called ningyo can change their fish bottom into legs. The earliest record of fishermen catching a ningyo dates back to the 7th century CE. In later years, spotting or catching a ningyo was seen as an ill omen.

Suvannamaccha is the daughter of the demon king Ravana.

Hanuman courts the mermaid princess.

SUVANNAMACCHA
The name of this Hindu mermaid princess means "golden fish." She appears in many versions of the ancient Indian epic *Ramayana*, including the Thai version. She falls in love with the monkey god Hanuman while trying to stop him from building a bridge to Lanka, the kingdom of the demon king Ravana.

This Yawkyawk figure made of palm fibers has the striped body and tail of a fish.

YAWKYAWK
The beliefs of some First Nations people of present-day Australia feature a creature called the Yawkyawk, who is similar to a mermaid. She can shape-shift into other forms, such as a crocodile or swordfish, and control the weather.

The magical herb also gave Glaucus the gift of prophecy.

GLAUCUS
Originally a Greek fisherman, Glaucus ate a magical herb that changed him into an immortal half-man, half-fish sea god when he leapt into the ocean. He often rescued sailors and fishermen from stormy seas.

The Chimera's tail was a deadly serpent.

A goat's head and neck grew from the the Chimera's body.

In Greek, the word chimera means "she-goat."

Head of a lion

HORRIFIC HYBRID
Chimera of Arezzo is a masterpiece of Etruscan bronze sculpture dating back to about 350 BCE. This famous depiction shows the monster's hybrid features and its pained expression after being attacked by Bellerophon.

CHIMERA
FIRE BREATHER

What do you get if you cross the power of a lion and the cunning of a goat with the poison of a serpent? The answer is the Chimera. This triple-headed, fire-breathing hybrid in ancient Greek mythology was a rampaging beast that devastated the landscape and devoured people to satisfy its enormous appetite. King Iobates of Lycia called on the hero Bellerophon to kill the Chimera and save the day.

ANCIENT GREEK COINAGE
Many ancient civilizations included famous mythical creatures on their coinage. Skilled artisans made this Greek silver coin called a stater in the 5th century BCE. It shows the Chimera on one side and a dove representing renewal on the other.

NUE

CLOUDY KILLER

One mention of this hybrid from Japanese mythology is enough to leave locals scared stiff. The Nue blends the head of a monkey, the limbs of a tiger, the body of a raccoon dog, and the tail of a snake. This ghastly shape-shifter can turn into a foreboding black cloud to fly anywhere it chooses. It also produces a sinister birdsong, and is usually seen or heard at night. Last but not least, any sighting of the Nue is a terrible warning of disease and death, with no chance of escape.

The wounded Nue falls to its death.

A wakizashi is a short sword used by samurai warriors for combat at close quarters.

SLAYING THE NUE
This woodblock print from 1820 brings to life a classic tale from 12th-century Japanese literature. Armed with swords and fire, brave samurai Minamoto no Yorimasa shot down the Nue from the roof of Emperor Konoe's palace with a single arrow.

The Nue is called the Japanese Chimera.

LOCAL LEGEND
This popular depiction, from a mural in Bavaria in southern Germany, shows a rabbit's head with a deer's antlers, a squirrel's body, and the wings and a leg of a pheasant.

WOLPERTINGER

CROSSBRED CREATURE

Not everyone believes in wolpertingers, but they don't mind because they are shy creatures that keep to themselves.
Wolpertingers are hybrids from German folklore that usually feature the wings of a bird attached to a small mammal's body. They live in the forests of southern Germany, and eat roots and herbs. They are not dangerous to people, but may squirt a smelly liquid when threatened. Taxidermied wolpertingers—made by putting together parts of real animals—are on display in many German museums.

TAXIDERMY
The art of taxidermy preserves an animal's body by stuffing the skin and head. Some tales of strange hybrids, such as this American jackalope (a jackrabbit with an antelope's horns), arose after taxidermists mixed parts of different animals in a lifelike fashion.

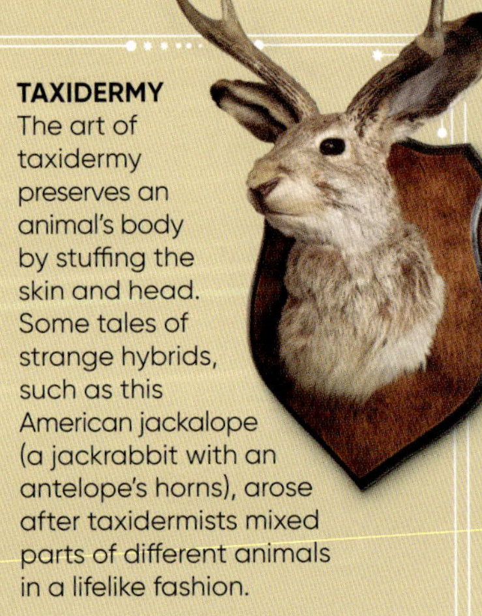

QUESTING BEAST

FABLED FOE

Many medieval knights set out on quests to find the Questing Beast. But only a few ever spotted it. This hybrid has the head and neck of a snake, the body of a leopard, the legs and tail of a lion, and the feet of a deer. Strangely, its belly makes a terrible barking sound, like a pack of hounds out on a hunt. It was first described in the 13th-century story *Perlesvaus* and later featured in English author Sir Thomas Malory's *Morte D'Arthur*, a 15th-century book recounting the legends of King Arthur.

This creature is also called the Barking Beast.

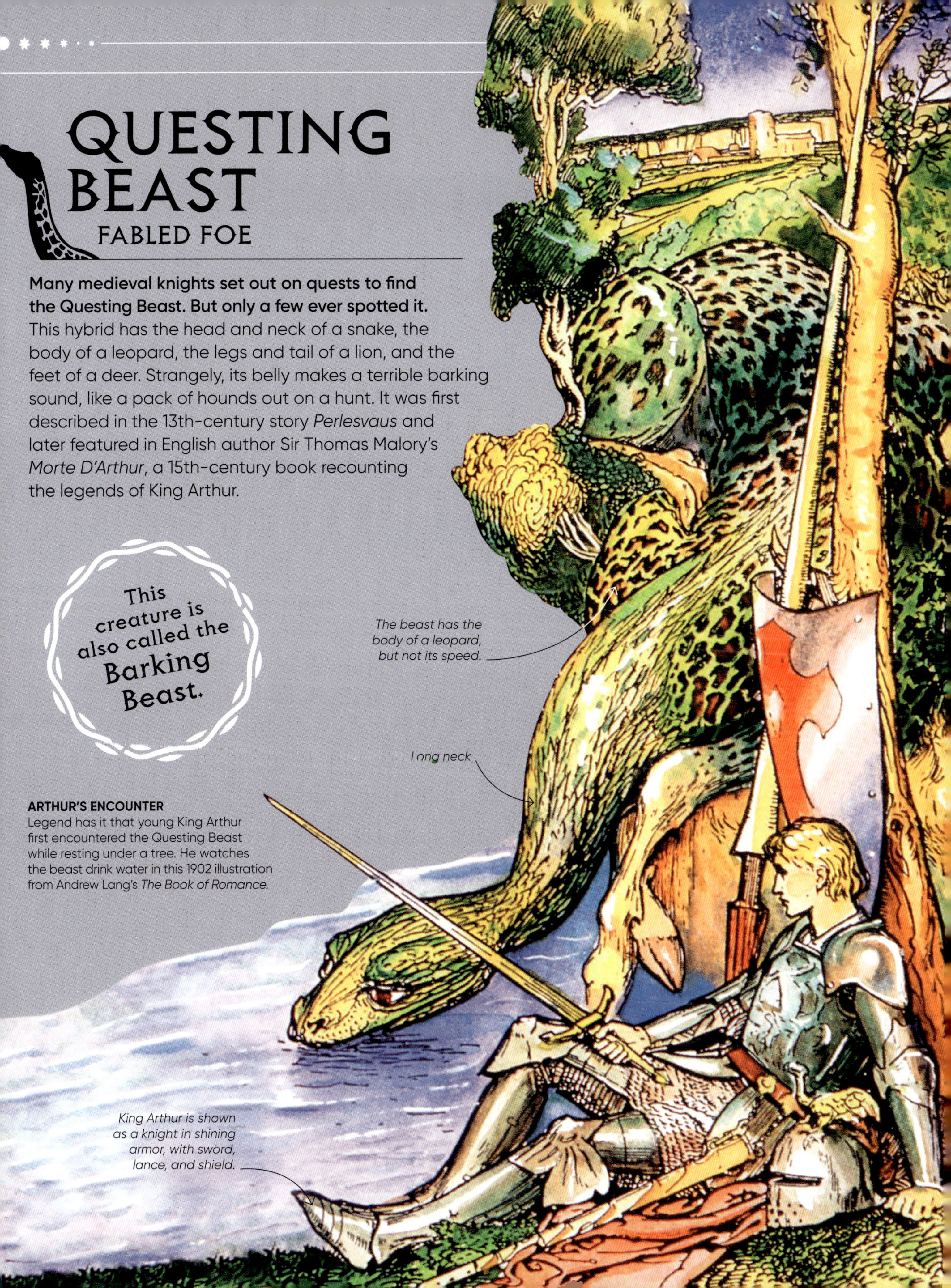

The beast has the body of a leopard, but not its speed.

Long neck

ARTHUR'S ENCOUNTER
Legend has it that young King Arthur first encountered the Questing Beast while resting under a tree. He watches the beast drink water in this 1902 illustration from Andrew Lang's *The Book of Romance*.

King Arthur is shown as a knight in shining armor, with sword, lance, and shield.

Helpers hold onto a pair of serpopards with leashes made of rope.

The entwined necks of these two serpopards may symbolize the unification of Upper and Lower Egypt.

COSMETIC PALETTE
The Narmer Palette from the Egyptian Museum in Cairo dates to around 3000 BCE. It is shaped like a shield and celebrates King Narmer's victory over his enemies. The serpopards in the central panel shown here are symbols of royal power and protection against chaos.

SERPOPARD
SERPENT LEOPARD

What do you get if you mix a serpent and a leopard together? A creature called serpopard.
Although this magnificent beast has been around since ancient Egyptian times, it only got its present name more recently, combining the words "serpent" and "leopard." Fierce and difficult to tame, it is often linked to the awe-inspiring power of nature, gods, and kings. This hybrid also shows up in the art of ancient Mesopotamia (present-day Iraq).

TATZELWURM

WHISKERED WORM

Beware the dreaded tatzelwurm that prowls the European Alps. This monster has the face of a cat, a serpentine body, and at least two or four legs, sometimes more. Up to 7 ft (2 m) long, it hisses and shrieks, and its breath is poisonous. Tatzelwurms prey on livestock in mountain pastures and attack people who stray into their territory.

GERMAN FOUNTAIN
The Tatzelwurm fountain in Kobern-Gondorf, Germany, commemorates the legend of the 14th-century crusader Heinrich Von Winkelried. He killed a tatzelwurm, but then died when a drop of its blood touched his skin.

The tatzelwurm's back is covered in sharp bristles.

Catlike whiskers

The long tail can lash a foe or coil tightly around prey.

Sharp claws for gripping and slashing

The beast rears up to intimidate victims or threats.

A tatzelwurm may hunt alone or in a pack.

ENCOUNTERING THE WORM
Over the centuries, several accounts have described alarming encounters with tatzelwurms. One account was illustrated in this 1723 woodcut by Swiss physician and natural scientist Jakob Scheuchzer. The Swiss name for a tatzelwurm is stollenwurm or stollwurm ("tunnel worm").

MOTHMAN
INSIDIOUS INSECT

It's unsettling to suddenly see a creature dark as the night, more than 7ft (2m) tall, with white wings and glowing red eyes.
But that's what happened to two young couples in West Virginia one cold November night in 1966. Other similar sightings soon followed, cementing the mysterious figure into a US legend. Was he a science experiment gone awry, or some kind of secret weapon in development? No one knows for sure.

The giant wings bear typical moth markings.

The large, bulbous eyes resemble those of a moth.

Cranes or herons in the dark may have been mistaken for the Mothman.

Big muscles show the Mothman's superhuman strength.

MOTHMAN MYSTERIES
Was the Mothman real or not? In his 1975 book, *The Mothman Prophecies*, UFOlogist John Keel discussed several unexplained events surrounding the creature. In 2002, the book was adapted into a horror-mystery film.

Clawed feet and hands

LOCAL LEGACY
When a bridge in Point Pleasant, West Virginia, collapsed in 1967, some people blamed UFOs and the Mothman, who was never seen again. Now this life-size sculpture towers over visitors at the town's Mothman Museum, where exhibits celebrate the Mothman's superpowers, reported sightings, and the Mothman movie.

JERSEY DEVIL

SCREAMING DEMON

In 1735, an American woman called Jane "Mother" Leeds was pregnant with her 13th child, but this was an unlucky number. Would the Devil please take it away?

On the stormy night Mother Leeds gave birth, the Devil heard her lament, and her baby was transformed into the Leeds Monster. Racing up the chimney with piercing screams, it was soon terrorizing New Jersey's Pine Barrens. As sightings spread across the state, the name Jersey Devil took hold.

THE DEVIL'S DETAILS
This 21st-century illustration conjures up some of the Jersey Devil's most hideously hybrid features—a large, horselike head; batlike wings; sharp claws; cloven hooves; and forked tail.

In 1909, a zoo offered a $10,000 reward for the Jersey Devil's capture.

IT'S BACK
In January 1909, people reported hundreds of sightings of the Jersey Devil. Published that month in the *Philadelphia Inquirer*, the photograph below shows a set of footprints allegedly left by the monster in Burlington, South Jersey.

WHAT-IS-IT VISITS ALL SOUTH JERSEY

GRYPHON

ROARING EAGLE

A gryphon has the front legs, head, and wings of a glorious eagle, and the hindquarters and tail of a lion.

Gryphons (or griffins) are noble creatures that symbolize divine power. These regal beasts feature in myths from a host of ancient civilizations, including Egypt, Persia (present-day Iran), Greece, and Rome. But they first appeared in Asia, as far back as the 4th millennium BCE. Many centuries later, gold miners and other travelers returning to ancient Greece from the east told of being attacked by gryphons in the Gobi Desert in Mongolia.

A pair of gryphons guards treasure in this 12th-century mosaic at a church in Murano, Italy.

HOARDING TREASURE

Gryphons have long been said to hoard treasure, including gold and gems. The ancient Greeks wrote that gryphons stood guard over gold in India and Ethiopia. Gryphons also pulled the chariot of the Greek sun god Apollo across the sky.

MAJESTIC HYBRID

In medieval Europe, the lion was thought of as king of the beasts on land, while the eagle ruled over the birds. This made the gryphon—part lion, part eagle—the king of all beasts and birds. It is shown in all its majesty in this tapestry from Switzerland, made around 1450.

Gryphons appeared in art more than 5,000 years ago.

SYMBOLIC GRYPHON

Gryphons appear in heraldry across Europe. They represent strength, courage, and leadership, and were especially popular with rulers during Europe's Middle Ages (500–1500 CE). Heraldic gryphons are usually shown "rampant"—rearing up with their front feet raised, and side-on.

This Russian medallion features a gryphon rampant under the imperial coat of arms.

COCKATRICE
DEMONIC ROOSTER

The strange-looking cockatrice has some impressive skills: it can breathe fire from its beak and kill you stone dead with a single glance.

It takes a series of unlikely coincidences for a cockatrice to be born. It can only hatch from an egg that has been laid by a cockerel or a rooster (a male chicken) and incubated by a serpent, on a nest of toad dung. Cockatrices began as an ancient Greek myth, were also called basilisks, and later became associated with the Devil in medieval Europe.

LOOK OF THE DEVIL
In medieval Christianity, the cockatrice was often used as a symbol for the Devil, who was the embodiment of evil itself. The Devil visits the bed of a dead person in this 13th-century illustration.

A cockatrice will die if it hears a rooster crow.

CHICKEN-HEADED DRAGON
The cockatrice is a hybrid that combines the body of a dragonlike reptile with the head, wings, and claws of a rooster. This statue is one of a pair standing guard at a castle in Croatia. They were created by an Austrian sculptor in the 19th century.

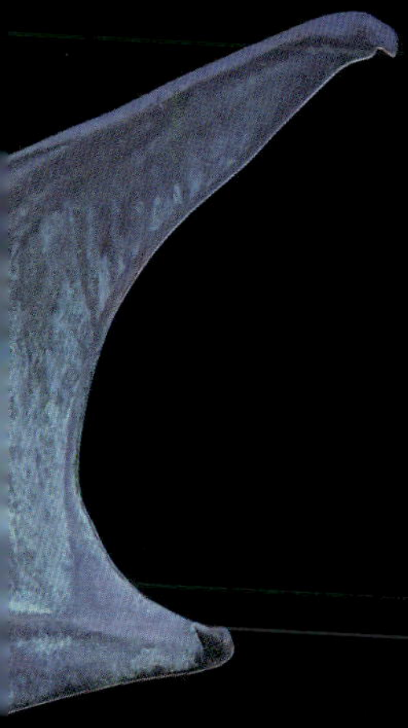

Colossal, eagle-like wings spread out behind Anzu's body.

MIGHTY ANZU
The Anzu's description differs across stories, but it is usually some combination of a lion, an eagle, and sometimes a human head. It appears frequently in ancient Mesopotamian art. This limestone mace head was carved more than 4,000 years ago, and was rediscovered in Tello, in modern-day Iraq. The Anzu was seen as a divine storm-bird, whose roar is the thunder that heralds life-giving rain.

The legs and talons are similar to those of an eagle.

ANZU
ANCIENT STORM BIRD

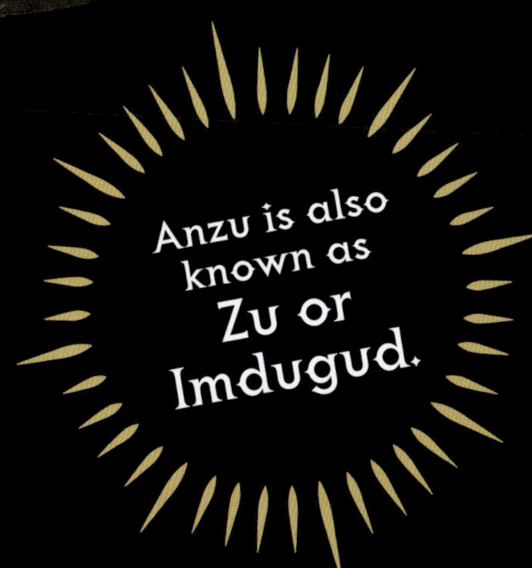

This ancient and terrifying demon has the body of a majestic eagle topped with the head of a fearsome lion.
The Anzu is enormous, with the power to summon thunderstorms and whip up strong winds. It first appears in ancient poems of Mesopotamia (present-day Iraq), written around 5,000 years ago.

HARPY
HOUND OF ZEUS

Terrible to behold, a harpy is a bird-woman hybrid with razor-sharp claws, which let it rip a human to shreds. The harpies of ancient Greek mythology are also called the "hounds of Zeus"—they are often sent off to do the king of the gods' bidding, punishing humans who have offended the gods in some way. The earsplitting screeches and overpowering stench of these wind spirits terrify all who see them.

EARLY ELEGANCE
While some later accounts of harpies describe them as hideous or grotesque, some of the earliest ones do not. In this statue of a harpy made in ancient Rome around the 1st century CE, it is shown with the face of a beautiful, long-haired woman.

The harpies are chased away by the Boreads, the king's immortal brothers-in-law.

King Phineus is helpless against the punishment.

POTENT PUNISHERS
The harpies were sent by Zeus to punish Phineus, king of Thrace (a region in present-day southeastern Europe), for betraying his trust. Phineus had used the power of prophecy given to him by Zeus to warn his allies of future threats, including those from the gods. Zeus made the harpies steal or ruin his food every day, so he remained forever hungry and slowly wasted away.

NAMING CREATURES
With its striking plumage and deadly beak and talons, the harpy eagle bears some resemblance to the mythical harpy. Some unusual-looking animals, such as the goblin spider, bluespine unicornfish, and vampire squirrel, are named after other supernatural beings.

In some versions of the tale, Kurangaituku's wings are even larger than those of an eagle.

In this artist's interpretation, the humanlike leg ends in a giant bird's foot.

NATIONAL LEGACY
Kurangaituku features in the oral lore of the Te Arawa and Raukawa peoples, but her stories are widely known all over New Zealand. This postage stamp shows the formidable hunter in all her birdlike glory.

KURANGAITUKU

FEARSOME BIRDWOMAN

Part woman and part bird, this cave dweller from Māori folklore once terrorized the forests near Lake Rotorua in New Zealand. As tall as a tree, she had a bird's head on a woman's body, with clawed hands and feet. When a man named Hatupatu accidentally hit her with his spear, she held him captive in her cave. He managed to escape, but she was boiled alive in a hot spring while chasing after him.

Kurangaituku is also known as a protector of birds.

SHAPE-SHIFTERS AND TRICKSTERS

Wouldn't it be fun to change your body into something completely different? Many of the creatures you are about to meet can do just that. And some of them are tricksters, who love outsmarting other creatures, playing pranks on people, and causing mayhem.

ON THE HUNT
All werewolves give in to their animal instincts once transformed. They snarl, prowl, and then run down their prey before devouring it raw. While some werewolves may travel in packs, most prefer to be lone hunters.

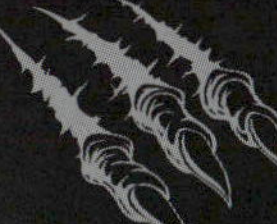

WEREWOLF

HOWLING HORROR

When there's a full moon, take care if you go out after dark. If you hear a hair-raising howl, run for cover—a werewolf could be on your tail. Werewolves appear in mythologies from across Europe. These sinister and terrifying beasts were once ordinary people, transformed by evil magic. After shape-shifting into a wolflike form when there's a full moon, a werewolf cannot tell friend from foe. Driven to a frenzy by a blood lust, they attack and kill anything that dares to cross them. If someone has the misfortune of being bitten or scratched by a werewolf, the curse is passed on, and they, too, will become werewolves.

MONTHLY TRANSFORMATION
A werewolf's aggression increases as the moon's phases change over each month, peaking around the full moon. This is when it undergoes a painful transformation from human to a wolflike monster that can stand on two hind legs or run on all four.

A werewolf viciously attacks a man in this 15th-century German woodcut print.

MEDIEVAL DEPICTIONS
Legends about werewolves spread rapidly during the Middle Ages, when wolves roamed widely in Europe's vast forests. Most depictions from the time show werewolves as actual wolves instead of the human-wolf hybrid we know today.

SCREEN SCARES
The first werewolf film to truly scare audiences at the cinema was 1941's black-and-white classic, *The Wolfman*. Werewolves have since cemented their place in movie history, in films such as 1961's *La Nuit du Loup-Garou* ("The Night of the Werewolf"), 1984's *The Company of Wolves*, and many others.

FIGHTING A WEREWOLF
Werewolves are impervious to many conventional weapons, which makes fighting them very difficult. Fire is one possible defense, but they are also vulnerable to silver, and can be wounded by silver bullets.

Silver-tipped bullet

EL PEUCHEN

VAMPIRIC WHISTLER

If you hear a strange whistling sound in the depths of Chile's ancient rainforests, you may be in danger of losing your blood.

The eerie sound is made by El Peuchen, a fantastic vampire-like creature that drinks the blood of its victims and features in the folklore of the Mapuche people from Chile and Argentina. This shape-shifter often takes the form of a winged snake. If it cannot find a convenient human victim, it will drink sheep's blood.

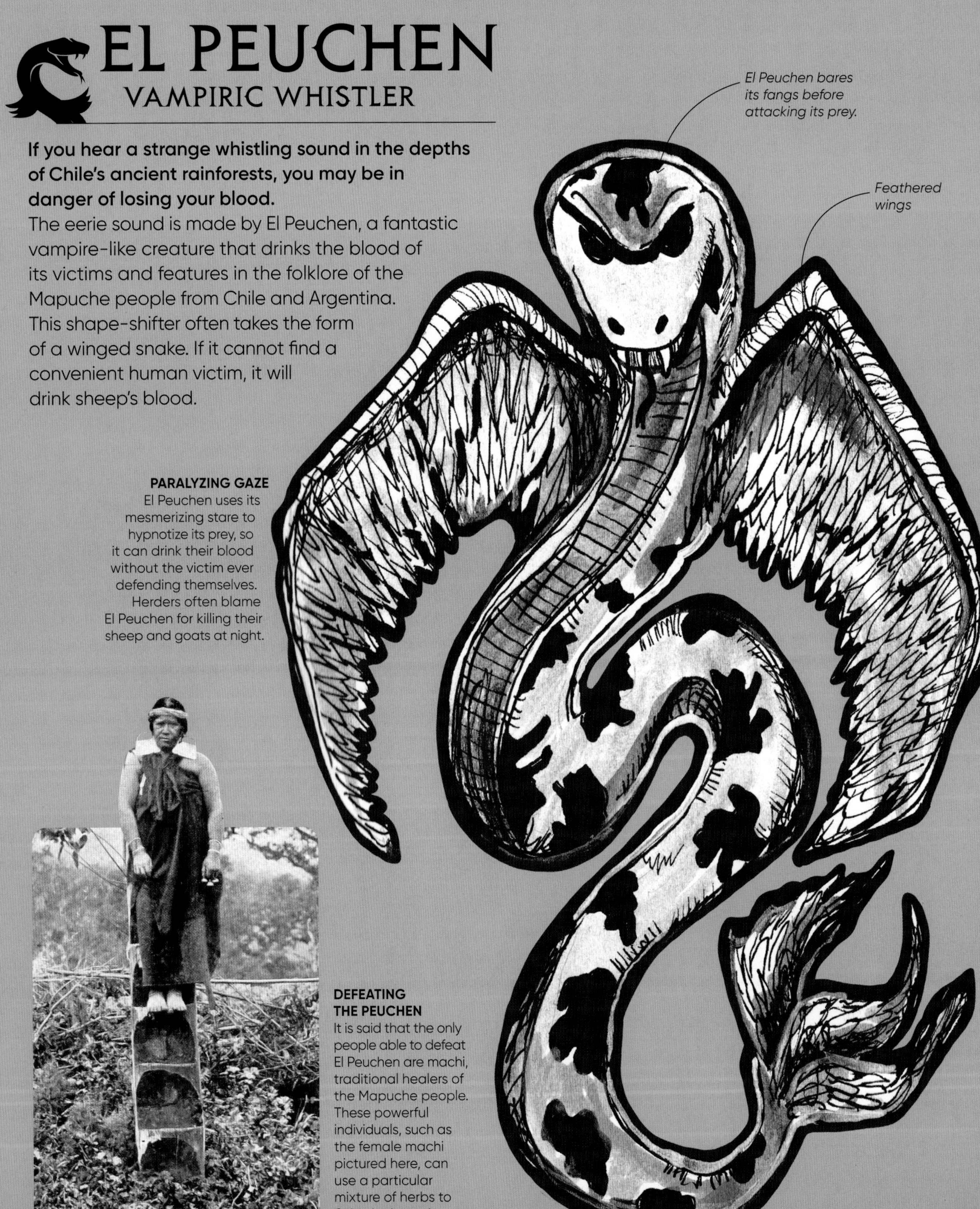

PARALYZING GAZE
El Peuchen uses its mesmerizing stare to hypnotize its prey, so it can drink their blood without the victim ever defending themselves. Herders often blame El Peuchen for killing their sheep and goats at night.

DEFEATING THE PEUCHEN
It is said that the only people able to defeat El Peuchen are machi, traditional healers of the Mapuche people. These powerful individuals, such as the female machi pictured here, can use a particular mixture of herbs to fight the beast's hypnotizing gaze.

A nagamani can be white, yellow, or even black.

MYTHICAL JEWEL

Legend has it that some venomous snakes, such as cobras, have a jewel called the *nagamani* inside their hoods. Pearl-like and immensely valuable, a *nagamani* can bestow huge wealth and power upon the human who owns it.

Three cobra heads flare up behind the nagin's human head.

CHANGING FORMS

This carving of a female naga, called a nagin, appears at a snake park in Chennai, India. Though usually shown as half-human and half-snake, a naga or nagin can change their form, shifting to become either fully human or fully snake.

Naga live in an underground realm called Naga loka.

This nagin is shown as human from the waist up.

NAGA

SACRED SERPENT

Powerful half-human half-snake beings called naga appear across South and Southeast Asia. Tales of the godlike nagas vary in Hindu, Buddhist, and Jain beliefs. They live in palaces underground, guarding treasure, but also in rivers, lakes, and wells. They bring floods but also fertility, and women pray to them for children. Some are shown with one, seven, or more heads, but others resemble dragons and guard gateways.

OLDER AND WISER
As a kitsune ages, it not only gains new tails, but it also becomes wiser and more powerful. After growing all nine tails, it is said to know everything about the world. This Japanese woodblock print from around 1850 shows a notorious nine-tailed kitsune who disguised itself as a royal concubine (courtesan), wreaking havoc in three countries—China, India, and Japan.

The red coat of a kitsune turns gold or white with age.

KITSUNE
FOXY TRICKSTER

Kitsune are fox spirits that have magical powers and can live for hundreds of years.
Unlike an ordinary fox, kitsune can grow a new tail every hundred years or so, and have up to nine tails. Japanese folk stories describe these creatures as tricksters, who enjoy punishing people who have behaved badly. Above all, they are master shape-shifters, able to turn themselves, other animals, and even people into giants, monsters, or—their favorite form—beautiful women.

BAKE-TANUKI TALES
Japanese folk tales often compare kitsune with another magical shape-shifter—the bake-tanuki, or raccoon dog. These creatures are even better than kitsune at transforming themselves into different shapes.

SACRED HELPERS

White kitsune serve as messengers and helpers to the Shinto rice goddess Inari. A Buddhist deity similar to Inari is Dakini Shinten, who is known to ride a white fox. Toyokawa Kaku Myōgonji is a famous Japanese temple dedicated to her. Behind its main building is a mound of white kitsune statues.

Armed with a wakizashi (a short sword), a court lady named Daji is possessed by the kitsune.

Traditional Japanese clothing called a kimono

A púca can turn into goats, cats, foxes, hares, and bears.

Púca may have extra-large ears.

REYNARD THE FOX
This sly fox is the hero of many medieval European folk tales. He is a coward, but uses his cunning to come out on top. In many tales, Reynard sets out to outwit other creatures, such as Chanticleer the boastful cockerel.

This 1846 German engraving shows sly Reynard is partial to dining on fowl.

PÚCA
Irish folk stories sometimes feature a shape-shifting spirit called a púca. Some púcas have human features mixed in with their animal ones. Púcas enjoy leading travelers astray, and ruining crops if they are not picked early enough.

This púca has taken the partial form of a horse.

Humanlike fingers, toes, and body

SACI-PERERÊ
This one-legged boy, who wears a magical red cap, is an annoying troublemaker in Brazilian households. He rides around on top of a miniature hurricane. He can shape-shift into a bird and even make himself invisible.

PAPA LEGBA
This character from the Caribbean island of Haiti carries messages between humans and spirits, and can speak all human languages. But take care: his messages are often given in riddles or dreams, and can easily be misunderstood.

This bake-tanuki has a raccoon head and human body.

BAKE-TANUKI
The bake-tanuki is the shape-shifting spirit animal of a Japanese raccoon dog. It has a large, bulging belly and enjoys playing tricks on humans.

SANG KANCIL
The small, timid-looking Indonesian creature called Sang Kancil looks like a mouse-deer. It is weak but clever, and uses its cunning to get the better of bigger, fiercer animals, such as tigers, crocodiles, and elephants.

TRICKSTERS
WISE AND WICKED

Myths from all over the world feature tricksters—naughty creatures who play pranks on others. Tricksters come in a huge range of forms: they can be a human, animal, spirit, or even a god. They possess great cunning and magical powers, and relish breaking rules and creating chaos. Some tricksters do this for fun, some are spiteful or downright evil, but others use their skills to help humans. They may teach people a valuable lesson, or come to their rescue, or provide useful gifts such as fire. These pages feature just a few of the many tricksters out there.

BR'ER RABBIT
Many West African folk stories feature a rabbit as a trickster figure—he is often small and physically weak but uses his quick wits to out-think larger animals. The character migrated to the US in the stories of African people who were enslaved and taken by European colonizers. In the US, the rabbit came to be known as Br'er Rabbit.

FEARSOME CAT
A bakeneko frightens a man named Izayoi in a scene from a play in this Japanese woodblock print from 1835. Bakeneko can pounce from the shadows at any time, and locals fear them, believing them to be an omen of death.

BAKENEKO
FIENDISH FELINE

Beware bakeneko, the Japanese cat monster with abilities beyond your worst nightmares.
This wicked yōkai (monster) can prop itself on its tail and run on its back legs, and even turn into a human. Its powers include haunting houses, throwing fire, casting curses, possessing people, and raising the dead. But cats have to meet certain criteria to become bakeneko, including being between seven and 13 years old, weighing more than 7 lb (3.5 kg), and having an unusually long tail.

SELKIE

SUPERNATURAL SEAL

While they may look like swimming seals underwater, on land, selkies can shed their seal skin to become human. According to Scottish and Irish legends, selkies have the body of a human under their skins. They are usually gentle, but can be vengeful if provoked. Selkies swim off the rugged coastlines of Scotland and Ireland, where they may be spotted by local communities and those out fishing. If a selkie loses its magical seal skin, it can never return to the sea again and must stay on land.

ORKNEY LEGENDS
The remote Orkney Islands off Scotland are home to all kinds of selkie stories—each of the 70 islands has its own unique tale to tell. The word "selkie" means "seal" in the local Orcadian dialect—seals can be seen near the shore, their heads bobbing above the water. Seal sightings may have given rise to the selkie legends.

SELKIE WIVES
A selkie rests on the shore in this 2016 painting by artist Gina Litherland. In Scottish tales from long ago, if a man enchanted by a beautiful selkie steals her seal skin, she is trapped in human form and can never leave him for her ocean home.

A child of a human and a selkie has **webbed hands and feet.**

SWAN MAIDEN

BIRD SHIFTER

In folklore across Europe, the magical ability to shift between swan and human form comes with certain risks. A swan maiden can turn from a swan to human form by taking off a swan skin or a robe made of swan feathers. But if this is stolen from her, she can be trapped in human form. Such is the fate of many swan maidens who find themselves held captive by human men. The stories of these maidens are similar to those of other shape-shifting beings in folklore, including the Irish and Scottish selkies.

VALKYRIES
In Norse mythology, valkyries are warrior maidens who serve the god Odin. In one tale, they are known as "swan maidens" because they disguise themselves as swans for a quick escape if needed. If a human man steals a valkyrie's swan feathers, even this fierce warrior may be helpless—she may have to marry him.

The ballet Swan Lake stars the swan maiden Odette.

MAGIC FEATHERS
After bathing in the water, swan maidens put on their feathered robes again in this 1894 painting by English artist Walter Crane. Other shape-shifting bird-maidens range from cranes in China and Japan to doves and vultures in South America and geese in the Arctic.

NAHUAL

PROTECTIVE GUARDIAN

In parts of Mexico and South America, people think of the nahuales as animal companions and protectors. Although European colonizers thought a nahual was a powerful, shapeshifting sorcerer, the Maya believe that a nahual is a spirit guide. Each person's nahual can take the form of a specific animal (such as a rabbit or a deer), object, or even a natural force such as lightning.

The **jaguar** is among the **strongest** spirit animals.

SPIRIT ANIMALS
The nahual in this image from a 16th-century Mexican manuscript called *Codex Borgia* is a deer. The word "nahual" means "disguise."

COLOSSAL CREATURES

Some supernatural beings may look vaguely human or apelike, but tower above us. They often live in places where we are less likely to spot them, such as in remote mountain ranges or dense forests. Some hide and sleep during the day, and come out at night when it is quieter.

Long, dense fur protects the Yeti from the cold.

YETI
ABOMINABLE SNOWMAN

There is plenty to worry about deep in the Himalayas in Asia—the cold, the wind, and the snow. But scariest of all is the Yeti.

This creature looks like a cross between an ape and a large bear. It is very tall, with long arms and legs, and is covered in dense fur that can be black, brown, or even white for camouflage in the snow. Explorers scaling the Himalayas have told of seeing this creature, but none has ever been captured. As the Yeti's legend has grown, it has taken on another name—the Abominable Snowman, while a similar apparition in North America is known as Sasquatch ("Bigfoot").

MANY VARIANTS
Tibetan lore describes three main types of Yeti—the largest is the fierce Nyalmo, which has black fur and can be more than 15 ft (4 m) tall. A pair of Nyalmo are shown in this 19th-century mural—the one on the right is devouring its victim head-first.

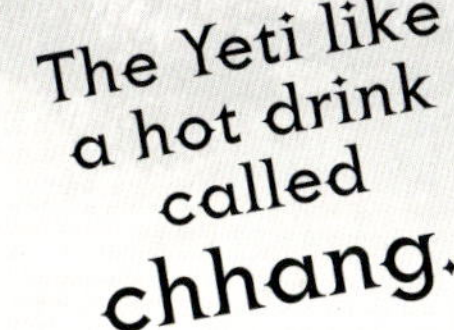

STALKERS IN THE SNOW
In this scene from *Monsters and Mythic Beasts*, illustrated by Gino D'Achille, explorers spot, and are seen by, the Yeti. Explorers have reported similar encounters since at least the 1830s.

FOOTPRINT SIGHTINGS
Although large footprints found in different places appear to match up well with the steps of a Yeti, no Yeti has actually been caught in the act of making them.

ON THE HUNT
Adventurers and researchers enjoy searching the world for mythical creatures—including the Yeti. In 1953, Sir Edmund Hillary became the first mountaineer to successfully climb Mount Everest, under the guidance of local Nepali guide Tenzing Norgay. In 1960, he set off on an expedition to capture the Yeti, but failed.

Hillary shows a drawing of the Yeti at a news conference.

Bigfoot's eyes may glow red in the dark.

ROCK ART
A Bigfoot family is depicted in this 1882 illustration by Walter James Hoffman. He copied it from an ancient rock painting near the Tule River in California. The rock art was probably made between 500 and 1,000 years ago, before the Yokuts peoples who live near the river arrived in the area.

The Yokuts word for this figure means "Hairy Man."

CAUGHT ON CAMERA
A creature many believers claim is Bigfoot was seen escaping into a forest in Northern California in a 1967 short film by Roger Patterson and Bob Gimlin. It resembles the Yeti in the Himalayas, and the "wild man of the woods" in European folklore.

ENORMOUS FOOTPRINT
In this photograph from 1967, filmmaker Roger Patterson compares his foot to a plaster cast of the footprint he claimed was made by Bigfoot. Such footprints have spurred on the hunt for the beast.

BIGFOOT

HAIRY GIANT

The North American Bigfoot lives up to its name, leaving huge footprints in its wake. Sightings suggest it may be up to 9 ft (2.7 m) tall.
Also known as Sasquatch, this monster walks upright and is covered with dense, dark fur. Although never captured, Bigfoot has been "seen" many times, particularly in the Pacific Northwest. Skeptics suspect it is really a bear, or an ape from a zoo, or a human prankster. Either way, Bigfoot has become a household name and the search continues.

SKUNK APE

STINKY PRIMATE

The Skunk Ape is hard to miss. Its awful smell, far worse than an ordinary skunk's, would give it away.

Although not as big as Bigfoot, this creature is up to 7 ft (2 m) tall, and covered in thick, reddish fur. It hides out in the forests and swamps of the southeastern United States, where people have been hunting it for decades. After one of the first sightings in 1957, many people claimed to have seen a Skunk Ape in the Florida Everglades, a vast area of coastal wetlands that shelter all kinds of wildlife.

IN THE WILD

The Skunk Ape "smiles" for the camera in this photograph taken in Myakka State Park, Sarasota County, Florida, in 2000. The sighting was reported by a woman who claimed that the monster was stealing apples from her back porch. No one knows the true identity of this nocturnal thief.

The Palm Beach Post

POSTER

WEDNESDAY, NOVEMBER 19, 1975

SECTION B

Waiting for Skunk Ape To Surface Again

Headline captures the local mood of excitement and dread in Palm Beach, Florida.

By MARILYN ALVA
Post Staff Writer

The Pacific Northwest has its Bigfoot. The Himalayas has its Snowman. And South Florida has its Skunk Ape.

Although there have been no Skunk Ape sightings for several months, those who believe the monster-like creature exists are convinced it will surface again.

Meanwhile, it is reported a movie is being made of the Skunk Ape somewhere near Davie in which the dark, hairy creature rapes a woman. Plans for the movie could not be confirmed.

Believers say the Skunk Ape, which reportedly lives in the Everglades, is a nonviolent vegetarian about 8 feet tall, with a stubby neck and muzzly mouth.

The Skunk Ape is said to have toes instead of claws and to walk on hind legs. Footprints have measured up to 18 inches long. Its foul odor accounts for its name.

The Skunk Ape was last sighted last spring by several youngsters in a wooded area off Gun Club Road in West Palm Beach. About one year ago a security guard at the Wellington Community Development off Southern Boulevard said he shot and wounded a creature resembling the legendary Skunk Ape.

Since the spring, however, police report no calls on the Skunk Ape. "We haven't seen him lately," said a Belle Glade police officer. West Palm Beach police and sheriff's deputies also report a lull in Skunk Ape calls.

Not deterred by the lack of concrete evidence — a Skunk Ape has never been captured — are Hialeah Gardens Police Chief Ray Bennett and Miamian Robert Morgan.

Bennett firmly believes there are Skunk Apes and encourages hunters in his district near the Glades not to shoot them.

What keeps Bennett going is an incident that happened seven years ago near his Glades area city of 3,000. Bennett says:

"We got a call one night to go out to 20-Mile Bend, where there's a trash heap. We had to subdue a little subject about 3 feet tall. Its skin was black and furry and it wouldn't talk. It just mumbled and held on to your legs. I decided before we got it to the hospital that it wasn't completely human."

Unfortunately, Bennett says, Jackson Memorial Hospital has no record of the "little subject." But since Skunk Apes have been spotted in recent years, Bennett says the creature he caught that night was "possibly a child skunk ape."

Morgan has been involved in expeditions to the Pacific Northwest in search of Bigfoot, as well as adventures in the Florida Everglades and swamps for the Skunk Ape.

Morgan used to say he was affiliated with the National Wildlife Association — and he was in a way — but the relationship soon soured. The association had administered funds to Morgan from a South Florida family interested in his work.

"We are very upset with this gentleman. We requested he never use our name again," said a reseacher with the National Wildlife Association. She said her organization was not pleased with the way Morgan conducted his investigation, but she declined to elaborate.

Morgan could not be reached for comment, which is not surprising since both Bennett and the Wildlife official say he travels frequently raising money and interest for his campaigns.

Bennett says Morgan's cause is justifiable and thinks of him as a "highly intelligent scientist or ecology man."

"He claimed he found some footprints and he got three hairs from this monster," Bennett says. Bennett says the hairs were retrieved from an automobile that hit the Skunk Ape several months ago near the Jones Fish Camp in Dade County.

The driver said he hit "a big, black monster." his report led to a search of the area by about 10 police officers and a helicopter. The creature never was found.

Bennett says he "still goes out occasionally and

The Skunk Ape hides in muddy, abandoned alligator caves.

MAKING NEWS

This 1975 article in a Florida newspaper reviewed the history of the Skunk Ape, and revisited well-known sightings, many of which took place in the 1960s and early 1970s. Urban legends continue to intrigue and baffle Skunk Ape's followers.

CORMORAN

CALLOUS COLOSSUS

Taller than a giraffe and angrier than a thunderstorm, this gruesome giant terrorized the county of Cornwall in the UK.

Legend has it that Cormoran built St. Michael's Mount, an island off Cornwall's coast, using granite rocks from the mainland. From his new base, Cormoran raided villages to snatch their livestock and children, stopping at nothing to satisfy his ravenous appetite. The giant was finally killed by a local boy named Jack.

A boulder marks the giant's grave to this day.

The giant was 18 ft (5.5 m) tall.

The giant carried off sheep and pigs, too.

CATTLE THIEF

Cormoran wreaked havoc by eating all the livestock he could steal from farms. In 1898, Irish artist Hugh Thomson pictured him stealing cattle in this illustration for the story, *Jack The Giant Killer*.

FALLEN GIANT

The final showdown between Gogmagog and the Trojan commander Corineus is depicted in this scene from a mid-15th century manuscript, although it is an older tale. Their wrestling match ended when Corineus threw Gogmagog to his doom over a Devon clifftop, which is called Giant's Leap to this day.

Shown here in medieval garb, Corineus became the first ruler of Cornwall, which was named after him.

GOGMAGOG

BRITAIN'S LAST GIANT

The rise and fall of this hulk is one of the earliest recorded medieval myths in southwestern UK. In the distant past, Britain was known as the island of Albion, a land once dominated by giants. An invasion by forces from the ancient city of Troy wiped out all the giants, but their gargantuan chieftain Gogmagog fought to the bitter end. He was twice the height of a man, and his courage and immeasurable strength ensured he was the last to fall.

PROTECTING LONDON

Gog and Magog are the traditional guardians of the City of London, These huge wicker effigies of the two giants tower over the parade at the annual Lord Mayor's Show.

GERYON
THREE-HEADED GIANT

The mythical ancient Greek island of Erytheia was once ruled over by the fearsome triple-bodied, winged giant Geryon. This giant was the proud owner of a herd of beautiful red cattle, which he guarded fiercely with the help of his two-headed hound Orthus. He was finally killed by a poisoned arrow shot by the legendary hero Hercules, who had been ordered to steal the cattle as part of his Twelve Labors.

READY TO FIGHT
This terra-cotta figure was made in Cyprus, in around 600 BCE. It may represent Geryon, and would have originally had three spears and three shields.

A helmet protects each head.

The only surviving shield

Geryon was the grandson of the snake-haired gorgon Medusa.

BLEMMYE

HEADLESS HUMAN

The blemmyes are fierce warriors who look much like humans, but with one crucial difference: they have no heads.

Instead, their faces are on their chests. Sometimes, they can have only one huge leg or eyes on the top of their shoulders. Blemmyes are tall—up to 12 ft (3.6 m) even without heads. They first appear in myths from ancient Greece, where they are said to live in North Africa. The ancient Greek historian Herodotus recorded that the blemmyes could be found in Libya.

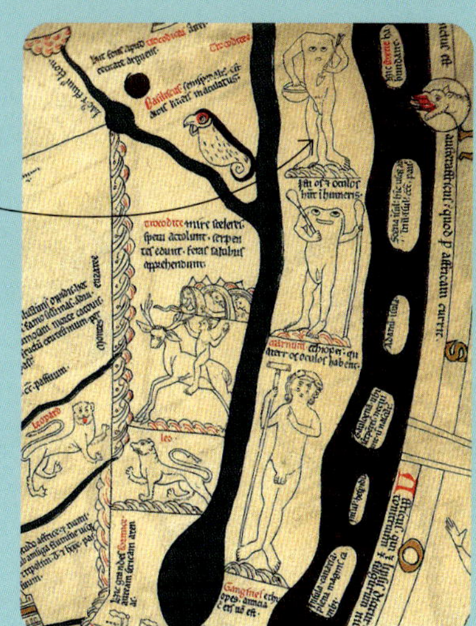

Two blemmyes can be seen on the map.

ON THE MAP
Sightings of the blemmyes were widely reported by medieval travelers and mapmakers. The Hereford Map of the World drawn in 1280 shows them south of the Nile River.

African palm trees

Emperor Alexander arrives with his troops.

Golden beards grow down to the blemmyes' knees.

A ROYAL MEETING
The blemmyes meet Alexander the Great, an ancient Macedonian emperor, in this scene from a 15th-century French manuscript. Alexander lived around 356–323 BCE, nearly 1,800 years before this artwork was made.

FIND OUT MORE

The supernatural creatures you have read about so far are only a sample of the many that are out there. Here's a quick look at a few more from around the world that are just as fascinating.

ADZE
Ghana, Togo
When darkness falls, the sinister adze shape-shift into fireflies or mosquitoes and set out on a hunt for fresh blood. They may slip through holes and cracks in the walls of homes, before biting a human victim and feeding on their blood, which may make their victim ill. The fear of disease spread by mosquitoes may have sparked stories of the adze among the Ewe people.

Adze

OBAYIFO
Ghana
The Ashanti people fear the obayifo for their insatiable appetite. These shapeshifting, vampire-like beings take flight at night to devour crops and drain the life force from children—which may stretch out over painful days or weeks until the victim finally dies.

ELOKO
Democratic Republic of the Congo
If you hear the chime of a bell deep inside a forest, then run, or you might encounter a dwarflike monster called an eloko. It lives inside tree trunks where it guards its food, including fruit and animals it has killed. But it may not need much persuasion to hunt and swallow unsuspecting travelers.

NINKI NANKA
West Africa
The swamps of West Africa are home to ninki nanka—colossal hybrids that can look like a mix of many animals, including a crocodile, a giraffe, and a serpent. These reptilian beasts may be up to 30 ft (9 m) long.

SOUL EATER
West Africa
Many people, including the Hausa of Nigeria, are terrified of soul eaters—supernatural creatures that consume a person's soul, which may lead to disease and death.

IMPUNDULU
South Africa
The beating of this immortal bird's wings produces claps of thunder. Impundulu feast on the blood of humans, and love to hunt children.

ROMPO
Zimbabwe
Don't worry if you encounter a rompo. It does not like to eat living things, and instead hungers for dead bodies. These hybrids have the legs of a bear, the arms of a badger, and the ears of a human.

WEREHYENA
East Africa
In many remote settlements in the East African highlands, people return home before sunset. Hungry hyenas can be heard cackling in the distance, so anxious parents warn their children about werehyenas. These shape-shifters can transform from human to hyena at night, and may attack people who've wandered off in the dark.

ALMAS
Central Asia
Like the Yeti and Bigfoot, the almas are hairy apelike creatures. They are about 6 ft (2 m) tall, walk upright, and weigh up to 500 lb (225 kg). People have spotted almas since at least the 15th century.

CHAMROSH
Persia (present-day Iran)
The Chamrosh is a defender of Persia. This giant bird has the head and wings of an eagle and the body of a dog. It attacks those who invade Persia, carrying them away.

Ninki nanka

GURUMAPA
Nepal
A terrifying giant with long fangs called Gurumapa once terrorized the lanes of Nepal's capital, Kathmandu. But villagers in Tundikhel, a place in the capital, still leave food out for it on a full moon night during Holi, the annual Hindu festival of color.

PIXIU
China
This bringer of good fortune is a hybrid—it has the head and wings of a dragon and the body of a horse. The Pixiu has a special diet—it loves to eat gold, silver, and jewels.

MANDURUGO
Philippines
This winged bloodsucker can drain the blood of sleeping men. When one man dies, she finds another.

Mandurugo

MANANANGGAL
Philippines
A manananggal may look like a beautiful woman by day, but transforms into a monster at night. Very few supernatural creatures have the power to split their body in half, but she does. After the split, her upper half flies off in search of food—usually the blood of unborn babies.

MRENH KONGVEAL
Cambodia
What is as small as a child and can only be seen by children? The mrenh kongveal. These elf-like beings are guardians of the forest, and take special care of animals like buffalo and elephants that travel in herds.

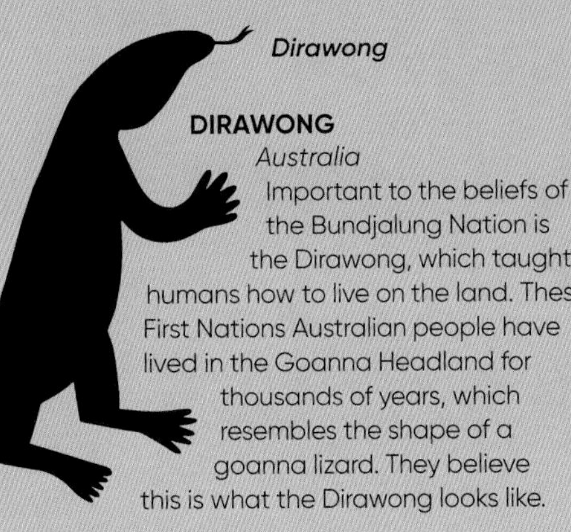
Dirawong

DIRAWONG
Australia
Important to the beliefs of the Bundjalung Nation is the Dirawong, which taught humans how to live on the land. These First Nations Australian people have lived in the Goanna Headland for thousands of years, which resembles the shape of a goanna lizard. They believe this is what the Dirawong looks like.

YARA-MA-YHA-WHO
Australia
A small yara-ma-yha-who can open its mouth wide enough to swallow a human, but only after it has sucked their blood. These little beasts hide among the leaves of a fig tree, waiting to ambush unlucky victims passing by, who are surprised when yara-ma-yha-who pounce on them.

ABHARTACH
Ireland
If you live in Northern Ireland, especially in Glenullin, stay vigilant for the Abhartach. This cruel chieftain from the 5th century turned into a vampire-like being who rises from his grave and comes looking for a bowl of blood to nourish his corpse.

CAT SÌTH
Scotland, Ireland
A cat sith (or sí in Ireland) is a fairy in the form of a black cat. As big as a dog, it can be a menacing sight with its arched back and erect fur. When humans aren't watching, these creatures can walk on two legs. They may be seen near burial sites, trying to steal people's souls after they die.

Cat sith

THE GREEN LADY
Scotland
The spirit of a young woman cradling a baby has been seen at Crathes Castle in the town of Banchory for centuries. Named after the color of the dress she wears, the Green Lady remains a mystery—no one really knows who she is.

BIG GRAY MAN
Scotland
This 10-ft (3-m) tall creature has dark hair and long hands. It is known locally as Am Fear Liath Mòr, or the Big Gray Man of MacDui—it haunts the summit of Mount Ben MacDui in the Cairngorms mountain range.

BEAST OF BODMIN
England
The Beast of Bodmin is a panther-like creature with very sharp teeth and white-yellow eyes that stalks the foggy Bodmin moor of Cornwall. It preys on local livestock.

EL COCO
Portugal
The dreaded El Coco can take many forms. It may look like a hooded man, a dark giant, or even a dragon, but its only goal is to steal children who misbehave.

LAMIA
Greece
This demon with a frightening face has a taste for human blood, especially baby blood. Lamia is a hybrid—she is half human and half serpent.

RATATOSKR
Scandinavia
In Norse mythology, Ratatoskr is a squirrel that relays messages between the wise eagle at the top of the World Tree, Yggdrasil, and the evil serpent Níðhöggr wrapped around its roots.

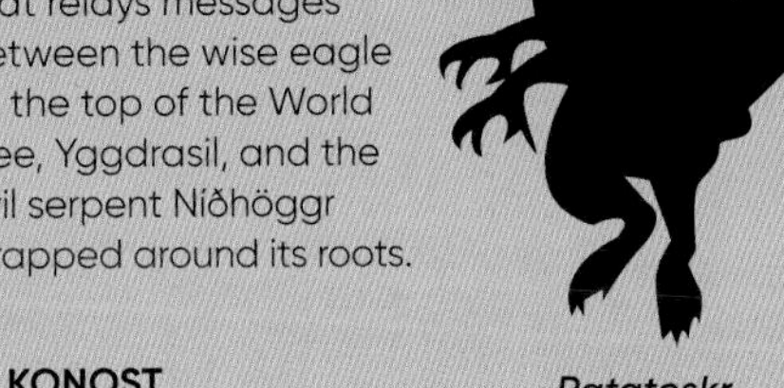
Ratatoskr

ALKONOST
Russia
The alkonost is a bird with the upper body of a woman. In Russian and other Slavic folklore, her magical voice enchants anyone who hears it, making them lose control of their actions.

GALLINIPPER
US
This hawk-sized creature from Black American folklore looks and hunts like a giant mosquito. Its stinger can easily slice through a man's arm and suck out all of his blood in a single gulp.

QALUPALIK
North America
Inuit children in the far north are told never to wander close to the shore for fear of meeting a qalupalik. These human-like creatures with green skin and long hair live in the sea. They may abduct children to raise them as their own.

RAINBOW CROW
North America
The Rainbow Crow is a symbol of friendship and sacrifice in the beliefs of the Lenapé people who live in the northeastern US and Canada. During one freezing winter, he flew to the Great Sky Spirit to stop the snow from harming his animal friends. The Great Sky Spirit gave him a flame, but on his way back, his feathers turned black and his voice became croaky. This made him sad, so the Great Sky Spirit gave him the gift of iridescence—his black feathers now shimmer with rainbow colors.

SEVEN O'CLOCK MAN
Canada
Canadian children are warned to go to bed by seven o'clock to avoid the Seven O'Clock Man—an old man in a coat and a hat who might put them in a sack and take them away.

ALICANTO
Chile
The Alicanto is a flightless nocturnal bird that glows in the dark thanks to its unusual diet of metal ores. The bird emits the colour of whichever ore it has eaten, such as silver or gold. The metal makes the bird too heavy to fly.

KUARTAM
Ecuador
Many toads are harmless, but the Kuartam isn't one of them. It lives deep in Ecuador's forests. If someone makes fun of it, the creature turns into a jaguar and eats them.

ASEMA
Suriname
These old vampiric beings remove their skin at night to shapeshift into a ball of blue light. Then they slip into people's homes to drink their blood.

PISHTACO
Peru, Bolivia
Unlike a vampire, the human-looking pishtaco doesn't suck blood from its victims—it sucks out the fat instead, killing its prey in the process. Pishtacos target anyone careless enough to venture out alone at night.

MAPINGUARI
Brazil
Lurking in the dense rainforests of the Amazon are these giant beasts with thick fur, long claws, and a gaping mouth on the belly, which they like to keep full.

EINTYKÁRA
Paraguay
This magical bee may not have a sting, but it produces a golden honey that can make you lose control over your actions or see things that aren't there. When many eintykára band together, they can shapeshift into a human.

GLOSSARY

AMULET
An object or ornament that is worn or carried and is said to bring good luck, protect from harm, and ward off evil spirits.

APPARITION
The unexpected appearance of a ghost or spirit.

ARTIFACT
An object made by a person and often of cultural and historical interest.

BESTIARY
A collection of descriptions and stories about animals, both real and supernatural.

CAMOUFLAGE
Colors or patterns that enable something to blend in with its surroundings easily.

CELESTIAL
In the sky or heavens, or relating to the gods.

CLASSICAL
Relating to art, culture, and literature from ancient Greece and Rome.

COAT OF ARMS
A design displaying the heraldic symbols that identify a particular family, town, or organization. Originally used on medieval knights' tunics and shields, to identify the bearer on the battlefield.
See also Heraldry

CONSTELLATION
A group of stars that forms a shape or a pattern, and is named after something, such as a mythical creature.

COSMOS
The universe.

CREMATION
Burning the remains of a dead person.

CRYPTOZOOLOGY
The study of supernatural creatures—in myth, legend, and folklore—whose existence has yet to be proved.

CULTURE
Shared beliefs, practices, and a way of life unique to a particular group of people.

DEBUNKED
Shown to be untrue by scientific research.

DEITY
A god or goddess.

DEMIGOD/DEMIGODDESS
A being that is part human, part god, or was once mortal and won divine status after death.

DEMON
An evil spirit that torments humans, causing pain and suffering.

DOOMSDAY
The end of the world.

ELIXIR
A liquid potion that cures illnesses, or keeps a person forever young, so they never die.

EPIC
A long poem, describing the adventures of a legendary hero, or narrating the history of a nation.

FAIRY TALE
A traditional story for children featuring magical creatures and fantastic lands.

FIEND
A wicked being.

FIRST NATIONS
Relating to many Indigenous peoples that were the original inhabitants of a region. The term applies to several peoples in present-day Canada, Australia (including the Torres Strait Islands), and New Zealand.
See also Indigenous

FOLKLORE
A collection of stories, traditions, and beliefs from a particular community. It includes superstitions and beliefs that are hard to prove.

FORGE
A place where a blacksmith heats metal over a fire and shapes it to make different objects.

GARGOYLE
A water spout carved from stone to portray strange beasts and human faces.

HERALDRY
The system of using symbols and colors relating to a family's history to decorate a coat of arms to use on a flag or a shield.
See also Coat of arms

HOAX
A tall tale with fake evidence and exaggerated accounts of a supernatural being.

HYBRID
A being that combines the physical parts of two or more different creatures.

IMMORTAL
Living forever.

INDIGENOUS
Relating to people who are the earliest known inhabitants of a place.

LABYRINTH
A maze or complicated network of passages that makes it difficult to work out the right way to go.

LATIN AMERICA
A region in southern North America and South America that includes countries once colonized by the Spanish and Portuguese empires.

LEGEND
A traditional story from the past that cannot be proved to be historical or true. Legends often feature mighty heroes, noble rulers, and fantastic beasts.

LYRE
A harplike instrument with a U-shaped frame, played in Greece and other parts of the ancient world.

MANUSCRIPT
A hand-written document or book.

MAUSOLEUM
A large, impressive tomb that serves as the burial place for the dead, often for important leaders or noble families.

MEDIEVAL
A period of European history, also called the Middle Ages, between the 5th and the 15th centuries.

MILLENNIUM
A period of a thousand years.

MORTAL
A being that cannot live forever, and will die. *See also* Immortal

MYTH
An ancient story or set of stories used by early people to explain their world or things they did not understand. Myths often feature gods and monsters.

MYTHICAL
Relating to myths; imaginary, not real.

MYTHOLOGY
A collection or framework of myths, especially those belonging to a particular culture.

MYTHOLOGICAL
Relating to one or more mythologies.

NATURALIST
A person who studies nature—plants, animals, and other living things.

NORSE
Relating to ancient or medieval Scandinavia and its peoples, including the Vikings. *See also* Scandinavia, Vikings

OLYMPIAN
An ancient Greek god living on Mount Olympus.

PETROGLYPH
A prehistoric carving, drawing, or painting made on a rock.

PHARAOH
A ruler of ancient Egypt.

PHENOMENON
An observable occurrence or event.

POLYNESIA
A group of islands in the central and southern Pacific Ocean.

PRIMORDIAL
Existing at or since the very beginning of time.

PROPHECY
A prediction of the future.

QUEST
A long, difficult search or pursuit to find or obtain something.

REALM
A kingdom, domain, or world ruled by something.

RENAISSANCE
A period of renewed interest in art, culture, and science across Europe during the 14th, 15th, and 16th centuries.

SACRED
Connected with a god and considered worthy of respect.

SAMURAI
A member of a Japanese warrior class that existed between the 11th and 19th centuries.

SCANDINAVIA
A region of northern Europe that includes Denmark, Sweden, and Norway, and sometimes Iceland, Finland, and the Faroes.

SERPENTINE
Like a serpent or snake.

SHAMAN
In many cultures, a person who acts as a go-between of the visible world and an invisible spirit world, using magic and chants. A shaman has special powers to communicate with spirits and heal the sick.

SHAPE-SHIFTER
A being who can transform from one physical form to another, and back.

SHINTOISM
A nature-based religion of Japan that features the worship of ancestors and nature spirits.

SLAVIC
Relating to the languages or culture of the Slavs, a group of people from central and eastern Europe.

SOUL
The spiritual core of a being, believed by many to live on even after the body has died.

SULFUR
A pale yellow chemical element that gives off an unpleasant smell like that of rotten eggs.

TRICKSTER
A mischievous character who plays pranks on people and gods, and relishes breaking rules and creating chaos.

TRIDENT
A three-pronged spear, often associated with the ancient Roman god Neptune (or the ancient Greek god Poseidon).

UNDERWORLD
The mythical land of the dead, believed to be under Earth's surface.

VIKINGS
Scandinavian seafaring people who settled in parts of north-western Europe between the 8th and 11th centuries. *See also* Norse

YŌKAI
Monsters or supernatural beings from Japanese folklore.

ZOROASTRIANISM
An ancient religion from Persia (present-day Iran) based on the teachings of the prophet Zoroaster, or Zarathustra.

INDEX

Page numbers in **bold** type refer to main entries

ACKNOWLEDGMENTS

Dorling Kindersley would like to thank the following people for their help with making the book: Lizzie Munsey, Rupa Rao, Neha Ruth Samuel, and Fleur Star for editorial assistance; Lisa Jane Gillespie and the DK Diversity, Equity, and Inclusion Team for a sensitivity check; Syed Md Farhan for DTP assistance; Elizabeth Wise for indexing; and Caroline Stamps for proofreading.

The publisher would like to thank the following for their kind permission to reproduce their photographs:

(Key: a-above; b-below/bottom; c-center; f-far; l-left; r-right; t-top)

1 akg-images: MAD, Paris / Jean Tholance. **2–3 Getty Images:** Pictures From History / Universal Images. **4 Shutterstock.com:** mz nu (br). **5 Alamy Stock Photo:** Historic Collection (bl). **Shutterstock.com:** CrashikBandicoot (bc). **6 Dreamstime.com:** Jemastock (bl); Yevgenii Movliev (bc). **Getty Images / iStock:** 1001nights (br). **7 Getty Images / iStock:** gaga vastard (bl). **The Estate of Norval Morrisseau:** (r). **Shutterstock.com:** delcarmat (bc). **8 Dreamstime.com:** Al4k14 (bl); Quicksilver77 (c). **Getty Images / iStock:** Big_Ryan (br); CSA-Archive (cr). **Shutterstock.com:** ieronim777 (cl); Maryna Serohina (bc). **8–9 Getty Images:** Pictures From History / Universal Images (background). **9 Alamy Stock Photo:** CPA Media Pte Ltd (fbr); Historic Collection (br). **Bridgeman Images:** Look and Learn / Elgar Collection (bl); National Museums Scotland (tr). **Gina Litherland:** Selkie, 2016. Courtesy the artist and Corbett vs. Dempsey (fbl). **Museum of Archaeology and Anthropology, Cambridge:** 2015.249 (tl). **10 Alamy Stock Photo:** Heritage Image Partnership Ltd (tl); The Print Collector (tr); Ivy Close Images (ftr). **Getty Images:** Pictures From History / Universal Images (ftl). **The New York Public Library:** (b). **10–11 Getty Images:** Pictures From History / Universal Images (background). **11 Alamy Stock Photo:** Allstar Picture Library (clb); Alister Firth (fbl); Martin Thomas Photography (bl); Everett Collection, Inc. (fbr). **Burnside Rare Books:** Saturday Review Press (br). **Dreamstime.com:** Janaka Dharmasena (fclb). **Shutterstock.com:** Daily Mail (t). **12 Alamy Stock Photo:** Arkadiy Ivanchenko (bl). **Dreamstime com:** IRudall30 (br); Ljubisa Sujica (bc). **Shutterstock.com:** Kirill.Veretennikov (tl); mz nu (tr). **13 Dreamstime.com:** Kirill Smalugov (tl). **14 Alamy Stock Photo:** CPA Media Pte Ltd (b); Ivy Close Images (tr). **Dreamstime.com:** Kvasay (tl). **15 akg-images:** (b). **Alamy Stock Photo:** Art Collection 2 (tr). **Dreamstime.com:** IRudall30 (tl). **Shutterstock.com:** NDK Studio (br). **16 Alamy Stock Photo:** World History Archive (br). **Getty Images / iStock:** subjob (bl). **Photo Scala, Florence:** RMN-Grand Palais / Manzara / RMN-GP / Dist. Foto SCALA, Florence (t). **17 Alamy Stock Photo:** Heritage Image Partnership Ltd (tl); Historic Collection (r). **Dreamstime.com:** Denys Drozd (cl); Vectaray (tr). **18 Alamy Stock Photo:** mauritius images GmbH (bl). **Bridgeman Images:** Fototeca Gilardi (br). **Dreamstime.com:** Golden Shark (tr). **Shutterstock.com:** mz nu (tl); NDK Studio (cr). **19 Getty Images:** DEA / G. Dagli Orti / De Agostini. **20 Alamy Stock Photo:** Album (t); Scott Camazine (br); Arkadiy Ivanchenko (bl). **Depositphotos Inc:** MioBuono12 (cl). **21 Alamy Stock Photo:** The Picture Art Collection (tr); Charles Walker Collection (b). **Shutterstock.com:** evanesa (tl). **22 Bridgeman Images:** Pictures from History (bl). **Dreamstime.com:** Miky Yal (tl). **22–23 Alamy Stock Photo:** Penta Springs Limited (c). **23 Getty Images / iStock:** FangXiaNuo (tr). **Shutterstock.com:** MonicaJ (cr). **24 Alamy Stock Photo:** The Print Collector (cr). **Bridgeman Images:** Christie's Images (bl). **Dreamstime.com:** Vectaray (br). **Getty Images / iStock:** ulimi (tl). **25 Dreamstime.com:** Deming9120 (br); Marta Cwi Cahyana (bl). **Photo © Museum Associates / LACMA:** Gift of Leo S. Figiel, M.D. (AC1992.170.1) (t). **26 Depositphotos Inc:** MioBuono12 (cb). **Dreamstime.com:** Ljubisa Sujica (tl). **Getty Images:** Sepia Times / Universal Images Group (cl). **Shutterstock.com:** Alastair Muir (bl). **27 © The Trustees of the British Museum. All rights reserved. 28 Bridgeman Images:** Ancient Art and Architecture Collection Ltd. (t). **Depositphotos Inc:** MioBuono 12 (br).**Shutterstock.com:** Kirill.Veretennikov (bl). **29 © The Trustees of the British Museum. All rights reserved:** (r, bl). **30 akg-images:** Erich Lessing (l). **Alamy Stock Photo:** Historic Images (tr). **Dreamstime.com:** Data2203 (c). **Shutterstock.com:** NDK Studio (br). **31 Alamy Stock Photo:** Granger- Historical Picture Archive (bl). **Bridgeman Images:** Pictures From History (c). **Depositphotos Inc:** MioBuono12 (br). **Shutterstock.com:** Oleg7799 (tl). **32 Alamy Stock Photo:** Historic Collection (c). **Dreamstime.com:** Ana Santos (tc); Вталй Барда (cl); Tomacco (cr). **Shutterstock.com:** Gizele (bl). **32–33 Depositphotos Inc:** clairev. **34 Alamy Stock Photo:** gameover (tl). **Bridgeman Images:** Lebrecht History /Courtesy Sir William Russell Flint Prints(cl). **Courtesy National Gallery of Art, Washington:** Gift of the Honorable W.S. Stuckey, Jr. (c). **Shutterstock.com:** Gizele (bl); MonicaJ (cr). **35 Alamy Stock Photo:** Shiiko Alexander (bl). **Bridgeman Images:** Museum of Fine Arts, Houston / Gift of Miss Ima Hogg (cl). **Getty Images / iStock:** tmietty (tl). **Photo Scala, Florence:** Manuel Cohen (r). **Shutterstock.com:** NDK Studio (tr). **36 Bridgeman Images:** Dirk Bakker (l). **India Office Library** (tr). **37 Alamy Stock Photo:** NurPhoto SRL (tl); The Picture Art Collection (bl). **Dreamstime.com:** Ekaterina Dukhanina (cl). **Gabriel Perez Salazar:** (r). **38 Alamy Stock Photo:** Interfoto (tr). **Dreamstime.com:** Вталй Барда (tl). **Shutterstock.com:** MonicaJ (ca). **39 Getty Images / iStock:** Valerii Minhirov (bc). **Library of Congress, Washington, D.C.:** (t). **Shutterstock.com:** NDK Studio (bl). **40 Alamy Stock Photo:** Red Pagoda (cr). **Dreamstime.com:** Deiby Vargas (tc). **Getty Images:** Pictures From History / Universal Images (l). **Shutterstock.com:** MonicaJ (bc). **41 Alamy Stock Photo:** ARTGEN (c); CPA Media Pte Ltd (bl). **Bridgeman Images:** Ashmolean Museum (cl). **Dreamstime.com:** Tomacco (tl). **Shutterstock.com:** NDK Studio (cr). **42 Alamy Stock Photo:** incamerastock (b). **Bridgeman Images.** Fototeca Gilardi (cr). **© The Trustees of the British Museum. All rights reserved:** (c). **Dreamstime.com:** Alexander Konoplyov (tc). **Getty Images:** Heritage Images (tl). **43 Getty Images:** DEA / G. Dagli Orti / De Agostini (tl). **Library of Congress, Washington, D.C.:** (tr, bl). **Nationaal Museum van Wereldculturen:** Coll.no. (br). **44 Dreamstime.com:** Vectaray (br). **Getty Images:** Ashmolean Museum / Heritage Images (bl); Malcolm P Chapman (tl). **Shutterstock.com:** Dankol (tc). **45 Alamy Stock Photo:** BBM. **46 Getty Images:** Pictures From History / Universal Images (t); ullstein bild (br). **47 Alamy Stock Photo:** Art Collection 2 (tr). **Getty Images / iStock:** tunart (b). **Shutterstock.com:** NDK Studio (cl). **48 Dreamstime.com:** Daryagribovskaya (tl); Ljubisa Sujica (crb). **Shutterstock.com:** CrashikBandicoot (bl); Park Ji Sun (bc); HN Works (br). **50 akg-images:** MAD, Paris / Jean Tholance (t). **Alamy Stock Photo:** Xinhua (br). **Dreamstime.com:** Vectaray (tr). **Shutterstock.com:** Malivad Rahul (bl). **51 Bridgeman Images:** (b). **The Cleveland Museum Of Art:** Purchase from the J. H. Wade Fund (tr). **Dreamstime.com:** Ljubisa Sujica (tl). **52 Alamy Stock Photo:** CPA Media Pte Ltd (t). **Getty Images / iStock:** Fairywong (bl). **The Metropolitan Museum of Art:** The Cloisters Collection, 1947 (br). **53 Alamy Stock Photo:** Amanda Ahn (tr); Matic tojs (bl); Sabena Jane Blackbird (tl); Science History Images (tc); Zoonar GmbH (br). **Shutterstock.com:** MonicaJ (cr). **54–55 Cheffins:** (c). **55 Alamy Stock Photo:** Niday Picture Library (br). **Depositphotos Inc:** MioBuono12 (tc). **Dreamstime.com:** Kertu Saarits (tr). **56–57 Bridgeman Images:** (c). **56 Depositphotos Inc:** MioBuono12 (bl). **57 Alamy Stock Photo:** HBO / Album (br). **Dreamstime.com:** Jnbm (tr). **58 Alamy Stock Photo:** Michael Harder (bl). **Bridgeman Images:** Peter Nahum at The Leicester Galleries, London / Courtesy Chris Beetles Gallery (bc). **TopFoto:** Fortean (tr); Granger, NYC (br). **59 Alamy Stock Photo:** Historic Collection (tr); Stock Illustrations Ltd (tl); Volgi archive (bc); Jon G. Fuller, Jr. (bl). **Bridgeman Images:** CCI (br). **Shutterstock.com:** MonicaJ (cl). **60–61 Alamy Stock Photo:** Science History Images. **60 Alamy Stock Photo:** John Sirlin (bl). **Shutterstock.com:** NDK Studio (tr). **61 Bridgeman Images:** (tr). **Dreamstime.com:** Yevgenii Movliev (tl). **62 Bridgeman Images:** Dundee Art Galleries and Museums (cr). **© The Trustees of the British Museum. All rights reserved:** (tl). **Dreamstime.com:** Daryagribovskaya (tc). **63 akg-images:** (br). **Alamy Stock Photo:** The Print Collector (tr). **Bridgeman Images:** Archives Charmet (tl). **Dreamstime.com:** Vectaray (tc). **64 Alamy Stock Photo:** Betty Johnson (tr). **National Museum of Korea:** (b). **65 Bridgeman Images:** Look and Learn (t). **Dreamstime.com:** Toseef Yousaf (cl). **Averil Shepherd and calendarcustoms.com:** (b). **Shutterstock.com:** MonicaJ (bc). **66 Dreamstime.com:** Michal Knitl (bl); Dmitry Samorodinov (tl). **Shutterstock.com:** MonicaJ (cl). **66–67 Alamy Stock Photo:** Zuri Swimmer. **68 akg-images:** bilwissedition (t). **Getty Images:** Heritage Art / Heritage Images (br). **Shutterstock.com:** Ksenica (bl). **69 Dreamstime.com:** Vectaray (tr). **Stephen Johnson. Shutterstock.com:** Park Ji Sun (cl). **70 Alamy Stock Photo:** Robert Thom (br). **Bridgeman Images:** Look and Learn / Valerie Jackson Harris Collection (l). **Dreamstime.com:** Sylfida (tc). **Shutterstock.com:** NDK Studio (cr). **71 Dreamstime.com:** haris mustofa (cl); Vectaray (tr). **Getty Images:** Stock Montage (tl). **Jean-Baptiste Monge:** (b). **72 Alamy Stock Photo:** The Picture Art Collection (tl); Mark Waugh (tr). **Dreamstime.com:** Artizarus (bl); Kravtzov (cr); Vectaray (br). **73 123RF.com:** puzzler1986 (tr). **Getty Images:** Sean Gallup (br). **Old Czech Tales:** Mikol Ale, 1899 (bl). **Shutterstock.com:** NDK Studio (c). **74 TopFoto:** Fortean. **75 Alamy Stock Photo:** Hemis (br). **Bridgeman Images:** Look and Learn (tr). **Dreamstime.com:** Anastasia Mrishchuk (cl). **Shutterstock.com:** NDK Studio (tl). **76 Alamy Stock Photo:** Album (b). **Shutterstock.com:** HN Works (tl); NDK Studio (tr). **77 Alamy Stock Photo:** funkyfood London - Paul Williams (bl). **Dreamstime.com:** Irina Kononova (cl); Wektorygrafika (tl). **Getty Images:** Fine Art Images / Heritage Images (r). **78 Dreamstime.com:** Elena Kozyreva (bl). **Shutterstock.com:** Bakhtiar Anwar (br); graficriver_icons_logo (crb); Artilution (cl). **80 Alamy Stock Photo:** Album (bl); Lordprice Collection (br). **Bridgeman Images:** Archives Charmet (tr); Fototeca Gilardi (bc). **81 Alamy Stock Photo:** JJs (tc); Pictorial Press Ltd (cl). **Bridgeman Images:** From the British Library archive (bl). **Dreamstime.com:** Donpomidor (tr). **naturepl.com:** Barry Mansell (br). **Shutterstock.com:** NDK Studio (bc). **82 Depositphotos Inc:** MioBuono12 (br). **Dariusz Fluder:** (t). **83 Alamy Stock Photo:** Matyas Rehak (b). **Shutterstock.com:** Artilution (tl); NDK Studio (tr). **84 Alamy Stock Photo:** POL / BT (tr). **Bridgeman Images:** Lambeth Palace Library (b). **Dreamstime.com:** Vectaray (cr). **Shutterstock.com:** Bakhtiar Anwar (cl). **84–85 Getty Images / iStock:** il67 (background). **85 Alamy Stock Photo:** CPA Media Pte Ltd (br); Painters (bl); Charles Walker Collection (tr). **Andrew DeFelice:** (l). **86 Alamy Stock Photo:** Black Star (tr); Nicolas De Corte (cr). **Depositphotos Inc:** MioBuono12 (c). **Museum of Archaeology and Anthropology, Cambridge:** 2015.249 (l). **87 Dreamstime.com:** Oleg Palium (bl). **The Estate of Norval Morrisseau:** (r). **Shutterstock.com:** NDK Studio (c); Salieri (tl). **88 Chau Chak Wing Museum, University of Sydney:** MAMU.NHM4 courtesy Macleay Collections (br). **Dreamstime.com:** Alexander Mirt / Bunyips stamp series, "A Bunyip of Aboriginal Legend, designed by Jerry Morrison, copyright Australian Postal Corporation 1994. / Australia Post (t). **Shutterstock.com:** Nana Tee (bl). **89 Alamy Stock Photo:** Torontonian (r). **Bridgeman Images:** © Alessandro Lonati. All rights reserved 2023 (bl). **Shutterstock.com:** graficriver_icons_logo (tl); NDK Studio (br). **90 Alamy Stock Photo:** Arctic Images (bl). **Dreamstime.com:** Elena Kozyreva (tl); Luca Lorenzelli (cl). **Shutterstock.com:** MonicaJ (cr). **91 Alamy Stock Photo:** steeve-x-art. **92 Shutterstock.com:**

Eroshka (c); Vector SpMan (bl). **93 Dreamstime.com:** Avictorero (tr). **Getty Images / iStock:** busenda (c). **94 Getty Images:** Pictures From History / Universal Images. **95 Bridgeman Images:** (tr). **Dreamstime.com:** Christos Georghiou (cl). **Getty Images:** brandstaetter images (br). **Shutterstock.com:** NDK Studio (tl). **96 Alamy Stock Photo:** GpPhotoStudio (r). **Depositphotos Inc:** MioBuono12 (cl). **Dreamstime.com:** Krustovin Juniar (tl). **97 Alamy Stock Photo:** Todd Strand (tr). **Bridgeman Images:** Look and Learn / Elgar Collection / Bridgeman Images (b). **Dreamstime.com:** Creativicadesign (tl). **98 Alamy Stock Photo:** CPA Media Pte Ltd (b). **Bridgeman Images:** Mary Jelliffe. All rights reserved 2024 (tr). **Getty Images / iStock:** FoxysGraphic (tl). **99 Dreamstime.com:** 9comeback (bc); Anurak Anachai (t). **Harvard University Library:** (bl). **100–101 Alamy Stock Photo:** ART Collection. **101 Alamy Stock Photo:** Felix Lipov (br). **Bridgeman Images:** Israel Museum, Jerusalem (cr). **Depositphotos Inc:** MioBuono12 (c). **102 Alamy Stock Photo:** Album (t); Heritage Image Partnership Ltd (br). **Getty Images / iStock:** busenda (bl). **103 Dreamstime.com:** Vectaray (cl). **National Museum of Asian Art, Smithsonian:** Takehara Shunsensai / National Museum of Asian Art, Smithsonian Institution, Freer Study Collection, Purchase. **104 Alamy Stock Photo:** Penta Springs Limited (br). **Depositphotos Inc:** MioBuono12 (tr). **Dreamstime.com:** Annatv81 (tl). **Getty Images:** Electa / Mondadori Portfolio (cr). **The Metropolitan Museum of Art:** The Cesnola Collection, Purchased by subscription, 1874–76 (bl). **105 Alamy Stock Photo:** David Keith Jones. **106–107 Alamy Stock Photo:** Hirarchivum Press (b). **106 Dreamstime.com:** Pavel Konovalov (tl). **Shutterstock.com:** MonicaJ (tr). **107 The Metropolitan Museum of Art:** Harris Brisbane Dick Fund, 1965 (tr); Purchase, Christos G. Bastis Gift, 1961 (tl). **108 Dreamstime.com:** crafteroks (br); Yevgenii Movliev (l); Evgeniya Mokeeva (cb). **109 Dreamstime.com:** Biljanacvetanovic (bl); Spiro Vasilevski (br). **110–111 The Walters Art Museum, Baltimore:** Henry Walters, Baltimore, Walters Art Museum, 1931, by bequest. **110 Shutterstock.com:** AlphaVectorStd (tl); NDK Studio (c). **111 Alamy Stock Photo:** Natural Visions (tr). **112 akg-images:** (br). **Alamy Stock Photo:** Chronicle (t). **Dreamstime.com:** Spiro Vasilevski (cl); Vectaray (bc). **113 Alamy Stock Photo:** history_docu_photo (r). **Shutterstock.com:** NDK Studio (cl). **114 Bridgeman Images:** Giancarlo Costa (b); Pictures From History (tr). **Dreamstime.com:** Maryna Kriuchenko (tl). **Shutterstock.com:** NDK Studio (bl). **115 The New York Public Library:** (t). **Shutterstock.com:** NDK Studio (br). **116–117 Getty Images:** Science Source / Photo Researchers History. **116 Bridgeman Images. 117 Alamy Stock Photo:** BIOSPHOTO (tr). **Depositphotos Inc:** MioBuono12 (tl). **118 Alamy Stock Photo:** Associated Press (br). **Depositphotos Inc:** MioBuono12 (c). **Shutterstock.com:** Art 27 (bl). **University of Minnesota Libraries, The Kerlan Collection of Children›s Literature.:** The Illustrated Police News. Volume 40, Issue 1032. 1886-08-07. (t). **119 Alamy Stock Photo:** Michael Wheatley (tr). **Dreamstime.com:** Nexusby (tl); Vectaray (c). **www.GenesisPark.com:** (b). **120–121 Alamy Stock Photo:** Allstar Picture Library (c). **Dreamstime.com:** Janaka Dharmasena (c). **120 Depositphotos Inc:** MioBuono12 (tr). **Dreamstime.com:** crafteroks (tl). **Getty Images:** Andy Buchanan / AFP (bl). **121 Maurice Burton:** The elusive monster: An analysis of the evidence from Loch Ness , by Maurice Burton (tr). **Getty Images / iStock:** Christine_Kohler (br). **122 The J. Paul Getty Museum, Los Angeles:** Ms. Ludwig XV 3, fol. 89v, 83.MR.173.89v (b). **Shutterstock.com:** NDK Studio (tr); twelve.std (tl). **123 Alamy Stock Photo:** Historic Collection (br). **Dreamstime.com:** Vectaray (tl). **Getty Images / iStock:** sangidan idan (bl). **Harold B. Lee Library, Brigham Young University:** Harry F. Bruning Collection of Japanese Books and Manuscripts, L. Tom Perry Special Collections (t). **124 Alamy Stock Photo:** Doug Houghton NZ (tr). **Depositphotos Inc:** MioBuono12 (br). **Dreamstime.com:** Evgeniya Mokeeva (bl); Michael Williams / Courtesy NZ Post (tl). **125 Getty Images:** Ashley Cooper (tr). **Getty Images / iStock:** oleg7799 (tl). **Karen Lee Mungarrja:** (b). **126 Alamy Stock Photo:** Associated Press (tr); CPA Media Pte Ltd (cl). **Harold B. Lee Library, Brigham Young University:** Courtesy, L. Tom Perry Special Collections (b). **Shutterstock.com:** NDK Studio (c). **127 akg-images:** (t). **Bridgeman Images:** Archives Charmet (br). **Dreamstime.com:** Webtechops Llc (bl). **Shutterstock.com:** MonicaJ (cb). **128 Alamy Stock Photo:** Scott Sim (b). **Harvard University Library:** (tr). **Shutterstock.com:** LovelyStocker (tl); NDK Studio (c). **129 Depositphotos Inc:** MioBuono12 (cl). **The Estate of Norval Morrisseau:** (r). **Shutterstock.com:** AlphaVectorStd (bl). **130 Getty Images:** Pictures From History / Universal Images. **131 Alamy Stock Photo:** Science History Images (cr); Philipp Zechner (cl). **Getty Images:** John S Lander / LightRocket (br). **Shutterstock.com:** MonicaJ (tr). **132 Dreamstime.com:** Emkamal Kamaluddin (tl, c). **Shutterstock.com:** Jones Design (tr). **133 Dreamstime.com:** Macrovector (bc). **Getty Images / iStock:** Lim Guik Khuan (bl). **134–135 The Metropolitan Museum of Art:** Rogers Fund, 1931 (c). **134 Alamy Stock Photo:** azhar iqbal (tl). **Getty Images / iStock:** 1001nights (cl). **135 Bridgeman Images:** Dahesh Museum of Art, New York (tr). **136 Dreamstime.com:** Macrovector (cl); Mrnovel (r); Tuayai (tl); Vectaray (tr). **Wellesley College Library:** The music and musical instruments of southern India and the Deccan" by Day, C. R. (Charles Russell), 1860-1900 (bl). **137 Alamy Stock Photo:** Science History Images (tr); The History Collection (b). **Shutterstock.com:** NDK Studio (c). **138 Bridgeman Images:** Novapix (bl). **Getty Images:** DeAgostini (c). **Getty Images / iStock:** Taufik Nur Ardiyanto (tl). **138–139 Alamy Stock Photo:** Ivan Vdovin. **139 Shutterstock.com:** NDK Studio (bc). **140 Alamy Stock Photo:** Dario Bajurin (l); Chronicle (br). **Shutterstock.com:** NDK Studio (cr). **141 Alamy Stock Photo:** Greg Balfour Evans (tr). **© The Trustees of the British Museum. All rights reserved:** (b). **Dreamstime.com:** Arkadi Bojarinov (tl). **Shutterstock.com:** MonicaJ (c). **143 Alamy Stock Photo:** Ian Bottle (br); Michael Wheatley (tr). **Bridgeman Images:** From the British Library archive (bl). **Getty Images / iStock:** Lim Guik Khuan (c). **Shutterstock.com:** MonicaJ (tl). **144 Alamy Stock Photo:** David Lyons (cl); Mouseion Archives (bl). **Dreamstime.com:** Artur Kutskyi (tl). **National Diet Library, Japan:** (r). **145 Alamy Stock Photo:** Art Directors & TRIP (tr). **Bridgeman Images:** The Stapleton Collection (b). **Dreamstime.com:** Montree Laoseeku (tl). **Shutterstock.com:** MonicaJ (crb). **146 Bridgeman Images:** Luisa Ricciarini (t). **Science Photo Library:** Photostock-Israel (br). **Shutterstock.com:** MonicaJ (tr). **147 Bridgeman Images:** National Museums Scotland. **Dreamstime.com:** Vectaray (bl). **148 Alamy Stock Photo:** imageBROKER.com GmbH & Co. KG (t). **Getty Images:** Diana Haronis dianasphotoart.com (br). **149 Alamy Stock Photo:** Charles Walker Collection (r). **Dreamstime.com:** Vectaray (cl). **150 Alamy Stock Photo:** Album (t). **Depositphotos Inc:** MioBuono12 (br). **151 Alamy Stock Photo:** Image Professionals GmbH (tr); Reinhold Tscherwitschke (tl). **President and Fellows of Harvard College:** Swi 607.23 (b). **Shutterstock.com:** NDK Studio (bl). **152 Burnside Rare Books:** Saturday Review Press (bl). **Depositphotos Inc:** MioBuono12 (cl). **Dreamstime.com:** Emkamal Kamaluddin (tl). **Kathleen O›Dowd:** Mothman, by Bob Roach (r). **153 Alamy Stock Photo:** Matthew Corrigan (l). **Philadelphia Inquirer:** (br). **Shutterstock.com:** NDK Studio (cr). **154 Alamy Stock Photo:** neil harrison (cl). **Bridgeman Images:** (bl). **Shutterstock.com:** AlphaVectorStd (tl); NDK Studio (br). **155 Bridgeman Images:** Pictures From History. **156 123RF.com:** ahasoft2000 (tc). **Bridgeman Images:** From the British Library archive (tl). **Dreamstime.com:** Jasmina (b). **Shutterstock.com:** NDK Studio (cl). **157 © The Trustees of the British Museum. All rights reserved. Depositphotos Inc:** MioBuono12 (br). **Dreamstime.com:** Rennaulka (bl). **158 Alamy Stock Photo:** Lee Dalton (br). **Getty Images:** DEA / A. De Gregorio / De Agostini via Getty Images (l). **Rijksmuseum, Amsterdam:** (cr). **Shutterstock.com:** abakeagle (tc). **159 Alamy Stock Photo:** Neftali / Courtesy NZ Post (t). **Dreamstime.com:** Macrovector (bl). **Shutterstock.com:** NDK Studio (br). **160 123RF.com:** ztoalphabet (tr). **Getty Images / iStock:** gaga vastard (c). **Aidan Harte:** (br). **Shutterstock.com:** Miceking (tc); tristan tan (tl). **161 Dreamstime.com:**Excentro (tr). **Getty Images / iStock:** Volodymyr Kotoshchuk (tc). **162–163 Dreamstime.com:** Andrii Biletskyi (c). **162 clipartpng.com:** (ftl). **Dreamstime.com:** Rasica (b); Yevgenii Movliev (c); Tartilastock (t). **163 Alamy Stock Photo:** Everett Collection, Inc. (cb, fbl); Granger - Historical Picture Archive (cr). **Dreamstime.com:** Elaelo (br). **Getty Images:** LMPC (bc). **Shutterstock.com:** AtiRose (tc). **164 Inkeater:** (r). **Shutterstock.com:** PO11 (tl). **Wellcome Collection:** (bl). **165 Bridgeman Images:** Dinodia (r). **Depositphotos Inc:** MioBuono12 (cl). **Shutterstock.com:** MAHATHUN (bl); Strikerxp1990 (tl). **166–167 © The Trustees of the British Museum. All rights reserved:** (c). **166 Depositphotos Inc:** MioBuono12 (tl). **Dreamstime.com:** Nazarij Kushlyk (cl). **Getty Images:** Molteni&Motta / Universal Images Group (bl).**167 Dreamstime.com:** Magalie Ascoop (tr). **168 Alamy Stock Photo:** Granger - Historical Picture Archive (tr); Sergey Nezhinkiy (br). **Aidan Harte:** (bl). **Shutterstock.com:** NDK Studio (tl). **169 akg-images:** van Ham / Saa Fuis, Kln (tc). **Alamy Stock Photo:** Chronicle (br); Historic Collection (tr). **Getty Images / iStock:** Volodymyr Kotoshchuk (cl). **Tampa Museum of Art:** Lherison Debreus (Haitian, b. 1971), Excite Lakwa, 2014. Sequins and beads on board. 35 x 25 inches. Tampa Museum of Art, Gift of Ed Gessen, TN.2023.207 (tl). **170 123RF.com:** ztoalphabet (bc). **Bridgeman Images:** Christie's Images (l). **Depositphotos Inc:** MioBuono12 (r). **171 Alamy Stock Photo:** robertharding (tr). **Depositphotos Inc:** MioBuono12 (ca). **Gina Litherland:** Selkie, 2016. Courtesy the artist and Corbett vs. Dempsey (b). **Shutterstock.com:** Miceking (tl). **172 Alamy Stock Photo:** Art Collection 2 (b). **Bridgeman Images:** O. Vaering (tr). **Dreamstime.com:** Vectaray (c). **Shutterstock.com:** Veronique G (tl). **173 Alamy Stock Photo:** The Picture Art Collection (b). **Dreamstime.com:** Excentro (tl), **Getty Images:** Pictures From History / Universal Images (background). **Shutterstock.com:** NDK Studio (tr). **174 Dreamstime.com:** Daria Chekman (ca); Md Farhad Mia (br); Lar01joka (tl). **Shutterstock.com:** delcarmat (bl). **175 Shutterstock.com:** Md sahir (br); shrimpgraphic (c). **176 Bridgeman Images:** Pictures From History (bl). **Shutterstock.com:** Md sahir (cl). **176–177 Bridgeman Images:** Gino DAchille. All rights reserved 2023. **177 Depositphotos Inc:** MioBuono12 (tr). **Getty Images:** Bettmann (br); Topical Press Agency (cr). **178 Alamy Stock Photo:** Granger - Historical Picture Archive (bl). **Bridgeman Images:** Look and Learn / Elgar Collection (tr). **Dreamstime.com:** Rinaherald (bc). **Shutterstock.com:** NDK Studio (tl). **Patterson-Gimlin:** (c). **179 Depositphotos Inc:** MioBuono12 (br). **Dreamstime.com:** Daria Chekman (tl). **IMAGN:** © The Palm Beach Post – USA TODAY NETWORK (bl). **TopFoto:** Fortean (tr). **180 Bridgeman Images:** Look and Learn. **Shutterstock.com:** NDK Studio (tr); shrimpgraphic (tl). **181 Alamy Stock Photo:** PA Images (b). **The Bodleian Library, University of Oxford:** (t). **Dreamstime.com:** Lar01joka (bl). **182 © The Trustees of the British Museum. All rights reserved:** (b). **Dreamstime.com:** Vectaray (br). **183 Alamy Stock Photo:** The Picture Art Collection (tr). **Bridgeman Images:** Pictures From History (b). **185 The New York Public Library:** More English fairy tales, Joseph Jacobs, 1922 (b). **186 Getty Images:** Pictures From History / Universal Images. **187 Bridgeman Images:** Look and Learn. **188 Dreamstime.com:** Daryagribovskaya (bc). **188–189 Shutterstock.com:** Gluiki (b). **189 Shutterstock.com:** Gizele (fbr); HN Works (br). **190 Dreamstime.com:** Elena Kozyreva (br); Maryna Kriuchenko (fbl); Evgeniya Mokeeva (bl). **Getty Images / iStock:** oleg7799 (bc).

Endpaper images: Front: **Alamy Stock Photo:** Historic Collection c; **Depositphotos Inc:** clairev (background tree); **Dreamstime.com:** Elena Kozyreva ca, Evgeniya Mokeeva br, Dmitry Samorodinov fbr, Yevgenii Movliev fcr; **Shutterstock.com:** CrashikBandicoot bl, graficriver_icons_logo tl, Kirill.Veretennikov tc, Md sahir bc, Vector SpMan cra. Back: **Alamy Stock Photo:** Historic Collection c; **Depositphotos Inc:** clairev (background tree); **Dreamstime.com:** Elena Kozyreva ca, Evgeniya Mokeeva br, Dmitry Samorodinov fbr, Yevgenii Movliev fcr; **Shutterstock.com:** CrashikBandicoot bl, graficriver_icons_logo tl, Kirill.Veretennikov tc, Md sahir bc, Vector SpMan cra.

All other images © Dorling Kindersley